Other Books by Michelle Kennedy

**WITHOUT A NET: MIDDLE CLASS AND HOMELESS
(WITH KIDS) IN AMERICA**

IT WORKED FOR ME: 1,001 PREGNANCY TIPS

**THE LAST STRAW STRATEGIES: EIGHT BOOKS ON
PARENTING TO KEEP YOU FROM THE END OF YOUR
ROPE**

Gandhi was a Libra

Michelle Kennedy

Beacon Hill Press

Gandhi was a Libra

Published by:
BEACON HILL PRESS
Chelsea, VT 05038

FIRST EDITION
Copyright Michelle Kennedy, 2007
All Rights Reserved

ISBN: 978-0-6151-5268-4

To John

-Always-

Acknowledgements

There are many people to thank for their inspiration and their support during the writing of this book. In particular, I would like to thank Robin Amber who encouraged me, even when every other publisher said my work was too "dark." And to my husband John who told me to forget what anyone else thought and to write the story anyway. As always, I have to thank my children, who forgive me for being "testy" when I am at work on my computer.

Gandhi was a Libra

Prologue

I always considered myself a sane person. I mean, pretty much sane. I never heard voices in my head or did anything really out of the ordinary. Perhaps that's why I was so woefully unprepared for the downward spiral. People ask me now, "Didn't you know that something was wrong with you?"

If I did, don't they think I would have stopped it? Even now, I'm not sure I would have. We are brought up learning the difference between right and wrong, good and evil. How does one get to a point where the lines suddenly become so blurred? When wrong could suddenly seem not so bad?

And it wasn't a terribly long road to that point. One would assume that the descent into mental instability and dare I say criminal behavior, would take years to come to fruition. Maybe they did. Maybe my whole life I was building to that point. Maybe each poor decision, each bad judgment call, was really the top of the spiral staircase and each wrong road taken just another step down until I was finally going so fast that I tripped, fell and landed in a heap at the bottom. Then ended up there, where the cement block walls encased my rage in normality. A mental institution. My new home.

Janet, my roommate, had it much worse. Her wounds were obvious, although not easily fixed. She was an abused child and ended up a prostitute at

14. Certainly her rage and defiance made much more sense to the outside world. They certainly made more sense to me. She didn't talk about it. She didn't talk at all. But I heard the nurses talk. Any notion of privacy went out the door when you were there. It's funny. The nurses wouldn't tell you about yourself, but they'd tell you all about everyone else. They're not much different from us. The only way you could tell the difference between them and us is that they went home at night. And they wore nametags. We wore wristbands.

I was there for a year. I think. I was never very good at keeping track of time. I always admired those inmates in prison movies that kept a calendar on their wall in pencil, marking each day until they get out. Janet kept a diary, though she rarely left her bed. Every night after dinner she wrote. I was always terrible at keeping a diary. I would start one with the greatest of intentions and for maybe three or four days I would write in it, but then I'd forget. After a month I might go back to it, only to read over what I wrote, be horribly embarrassed by it and then rip those pages out - vowing to start anew with much deeper insights and quotations from my favorite writers.

I'd rather read. I've always read everything. Cereal boxes at the breakfast table, bottles of shampoo in the shower, books hidden in my lap during Geometry class in high school. The library there sucked. Tons of crappy fiction, Harlequin romances and the like. Nothing too provoking for the criminal minds among us. My husband went to the library in town and brought me new books every Friday.

I met with my psychiatrist every couple of days. It should have been everyday, she said, but this was a county facility and that just wasn't in the budget. She wasn't completely useless. Dr. Leslie Sherman. We could call her "Leslie," she said. She was so damn happy. I used to be cheerful like that - all of the time. I always put on a happy face. That is the one attitude attribute that always wins potential employers over. It's my little mantra.

"I believe the customer is always right," I tell them. "No matter what bad thing may have happened to me, I always bring a smiling face to the customer."

Sickening, isn't it? Leslie didn't think so. She put it on my list of "good attributes," but said we should discuss my need to not let anyone know what I'm really feeling. Whatever.

Leslie reminded me of the midwife that delivered my children. She wore those long wrinkly flowing skirts and bunched up rag socks with Birkenstock clogs. Her hair was long and gray and always wrapped in some faux-African scarf. Her office was kind of cool: big overstuffed chairs and Oriental rugs on the floor, books up to the ceiling. But it smelled like cat piss and there was cat hair everywhere. And she wouldn't let me smoke. But I never saw a cat. What does that mean? It drove me nuts, forgive the pun. I always felt like I had a hairball when I left there.

I didn't always smoke, but I liked it. It gave me something to do with my hands and kept me from eating. The Depakote made me fat and it's not like I needed any weight to begin with.

"Smokists," that's what Valerie called them.

We were sitting in lawn chairs out in the courtyard one day; smoking with the nurses and watching the speds play basketball, when she came up with it. The speds live on the third floor. They are the potentially violent mentally retarded. That's what they call themselves, so we just went with it, Valerie and I.

"It's short for special education," some guy named Larry told me in his thick, stuttered speech. "That's what they called us in school: sped."

"Didn't it bother you?"

"Nah," he laughed, "it was better than loser."

I couldn't argue with that. I wouldn't have even if I could because whenever you talk with Larry or one of the other guys from the third floor, there is always a big male nurse named Jim holding their hands down so that you don't get hit.

Valerie leapt out of her chair and swiped the ball from a big, brooding sped, who didn't see it coming. She raced to the basket and made a perfect lay up. Then she caught it, raced out to half court and lobbed another perfect shot. Valerie's energy was frightening. She couldn't be more than 20 and her perfect body and model looks would, I think, be shocking to anyone looking in. But she didn't seem a bit out of place.

She ran back towards us and plopped back down in her chair. She sprayed water from my bottle over her head and reached underneath her chair for another smoke.

"Yup," she said, as though our conversation had never stopped, "Doc Lesbian is a smokist. In fact, most people are these days. Do you know some woman actually yelled at me one day because I was smoking on the park bench I was sharing with her? I said, 'Lady, I am outside, in public, you can't tell me not to smoke.' And she went on about how I was polluting her right to breathe and all of this shit."

"What did you do?" I asked.

"I blew a big old puff right in her scrawny face and then she got up and left. I mean, for Chris sakes, it's not like she had a kid with her or there weren't fifty other park benches.

"What's even worse is there are bars now that won't let you smoke. Can you believe that shit? Bars. What am I supposed to do when I drink, eat pretzels?"

I was trying to think of an answer to this dilemma, but was rescued by our own Nurse McLaughlin, who blew her coach's whistle to get our attention.

"Alright ladies, back inside. Smokes out. Now please, Valerie."

Valerie flicked her cigarette onto the court. I daintily crushed mine under my Keds as my cigarette flicking skills left much to be desired. I tried to flick one once, but it went haywire and landed on someone's shoe, so I haven't tried since.

I hiked my scrubs up and tied them tighter as I followed the line back to our floor. As soon as we got inside, Valerie hightailed it for the smoke room so she could have one more before "group." Valerie was a voluntary commitment, so she pretty much got to do as she pleased. I was not. I had been dragged kicking and screaming into this place, or so I've been told, and I wouldn't be allowed to leave anytime soon. The Depakote made it so I really didn't care anymore. That's one of the best effects of being diagnosed with bipolar disorder; the drugs make it so you no longer care how crazy you are. I knew I'd get out eventually and right then, that was enough.

I followed the line down the puke green hall, obviously an homage to 70s industrial design, to the group session room. This room was painted red and blue in big bright blocks, as if one of the nurses had recently flipped through a book of Picasso's paintings and said, "that one," to a poor orderly. I flopped down into one of the dormitory style foam chairs and waited for the wailing to begin.

Our group counselor was Rick. Rick was approximately 10 years old and had obviously just gotten out of grad school. I was guessing this little tour of duty was his way to pay back part of his college education. I had only been allowed into group sessions a couple of days before so I didn't say very much. I liked to watch. As if some morbid reality TV soap opera was being staged just for me.

"Today we'll be talking about trust," Rick began. "Why do we trust? Who do we trust? Who don't we trust? In general terms, I mean. What are the characteristics of a person you would trust? Sheila?"

"I don't trust no one," Sheila said.

"Me neither," a girl named Rhonda added. "All trustin' gets you is fucked up. I trusted this guy once and he knocked me up, then he beat me up and left me. How's that for trust?"

Oh Rick, I thought, you've done it now.

"OK, OK. These are really terrible things, but what characteristics do you think a person you could trust should have?"

"Well, I would think that a person who told me he loved me and knocked me up would be a person I could trust, but obviously I was wrong now wasn't I?" Rhonda said. "So, I don't know - I think you don't trust nobody and then you don't have to worry about it."

Oh Ricky, this is out of control. Bring it back. My heart was breaking for the kid. He really was just dumb. This wasn't alcoholics anonymous for crying out loud. These women wanted to cause pain. They wanted to kill themselves, or other people.

But it went on and finally Rick got them to help him make a list of characteristics on the blackboard. Not wanting to seem too out of touch, I added, "good listener" to the list. Valerie never did make it to group. I was certain she could have controlled the conversation and come up with a hell of a list.

Finally Rick let us out and we filed down the hall to our rooms. Mine was a small room: two beds, two nightstands, without drawers, and a wall of cabinets without handles. The cabinets had magnetic doors and strange looking hinges that will prevent us, I am told, from hanging ourselves. The doors have these same hinges. When I first got here, I didn't have a room. Well, I did, but it only had a bare mattress on the floor, with only a blanket in it.

I was on 24-hour suicide watch. I was distraught, they said. I really only remember being sleepy. That, and one day it was a Tuesday and I was playing with my kids on the floor and the next thing I knew it was two weeks later and

I was in that room with the constant changing of bored looking people sitting in the open doorway, reading a magazine.

Like I said, I don't remember much else. I do remember the cold of that piss-colored linoleum floor. I remember the feeling of those stupid slippers they put on my feet, made out of terry cloth and too small. They didn't keep my feet warm. The blanket didn't keep me warm either. It was thin and gray and I kept catching my foot in the open threads at the bottom.

I was allowed out, but I didn't want to go anywhere. The first time I went to the bathroom, I caught a glimpse of myself in the mirror. My previously long red hair now short and sticking up and matted, my face red and puffy from crying. I didn't look in the mirror anymore after that. All I wanted to do was sleep. Sleep it all away. And I did.

In my dreams, I was at the ocean, relaxing on the sand while my children played in the surf and brought me seashells. That's really all I have ever wanted. Peace. Quiet. Not quiet from the noise of the children. I love their noise. Just peace from life and all its hideousness. A place where I didn't have to worry, where everything was just taken care of. Such a place did not exist outside the cold walls of this institution. I was starting to like it here and that thought scared me.

Chapter 1

A s I sat on my bed, composing my weekly, cheerful letter to my children, Valerie burst in announcing lunch.

"Carrie, Fido says it's time for lunch, get a move on will ya? I don't want to miss out on dessert again," she said.

"Just a sec," I said. "I want to finish this up and get it in the mail today."

"God, you are always writing," she said. She snatched the letter and read it. Her sarcastic look eased, briefly, and then she flung it back to me. "Just hurry up, will you?"

I sealed the letter and left it in the outbox at the nurse's station as we walked down the hall. Everyone was waiting for us in front of the locked doors. We had to go to the cafeteria together. We had to do everything together.

The cafeteria is crazy. Three times a day, all of the floors eat together. The only people who get to eat on their own floor are the nursing home residents. They're normal and don't have to mix in with the rest of us.

I followed Valerie into line and picked up a plastic tray. The meals were surprisingly good, all cooked right there by the kitchen staff. Big vats of mashed potatoes, spaghetti, mac and cheese, standard school lunch fare. The salad was the only thing that suffered. The wilting iceberg lettuce the only relatively green menu item and consequently everyone's tray had varying shades of beige and brown when they returned to our section.

I picked at my mashed potatoes and settled for a roll. It's amazing. I ate hardly anything, yet still can't lose a pound while Valerie consumes everything - including two desserts and is rail-thin. Sitting there, watching the nurses feed the men from the third floor, I was shocked that I still had some vanity left. What did it matter how much I weighed? It's not like I had a pair of jeans to fit into. Scrubs fit me no matter what.

As I peeled apart the layers of my dinner roll, I watched one particularly large male nursing assistant try and simultaneously train an obviously new employee and feed three of his charges, one of which was blind. The man was patient, with long dark hair and a long beard flecked with gray. His tattoos, black jeans and t-shirt made him look as though he would have been more comfortable on a Harley than in a mental institution, but he seemed at ease among them...us.

"Here Joe," he said, passing the blind man a piece of a cheeseburger. "Now Lillian, try some potatoes." And then he took away all of the food on the woman's tray and then placed the bowl of potatoes directly in front of her.

"Shut up," was Lillian's only response. But she tried some of the potatoes anyway. The man then spoon-fed a woman, who looked to have cerebral palsy, some pudding. He talked with the timid young woman at his side while constantly feeding each of the trio in turn.

"Now Lillian here is really a softie, aren't you Lillian?" he said.

"Shut up," Lillian said, spooning more potatoes into her mouth.

"She always says that, don't let it bother you," he said. "But Victor here is a little more interesting. You have to watch his hands all of the time. He can be pretty violent when he wants to be."

"Aw Dennis, that's not true," Victor said as he felt Dennis's hand for a cookie.

"Well, we all have our moments Vic and sometimes you have yours," he said. "But Vic isn't always violent to others. He's blind because he scratched his own eyes out when he was, what was it Vic? Twelve?"

"Oh, I don't know," Vic said, shockingly nonchalant about the conversation, "it was around then."

"That's so sad," the young nurse said.

"It's not sad," Vic said taking offense. "It's just true, that's all. OK?"

"OK," the nurse said. "I'm sorry."

"Whatever," Vic said.

"Shut up, shut up, good god shut up," Lillian added, obviously irritated at being left out.

The nurse looked around the room and smoothed her neat new uniform. Uniforms weren't mandatory here - no one wore them - but she obviously was trying to make a good impression and portray some authority. The young nurse caught my eye and stared at me for second. I smiled at her, much like I would have if she had caught my eye in the grocery store. But I wasn't in the grocery store now, was I? I was one of them and she surely pitied me. Perhaps she was even afraid of me, wondering did she have to watch all of our hands?

It looked as though the trio was finished and so the pretty nurse, who looked all of 16, began to gather the trays and cups and take them to the garbage can. That's how we did it, like we were in a fast food restaurant. And I had to say, I've been in a lot of fast food restaurants and the clientele here didn't look much different.

I watched as Dennis gathered all of his charges, including some I hadn't noticed he had. Others, I assume, who were able to feed themselves and sit with minimal supervision. Most were in wheelchairs and those who weren't had walkers. He and the nurse took them one by one to the elevator where they waited in a long line to get to their place on the third floor.

"Aren't you going to eat anything?" Valerie was leaning across the table and peering at me about three inches from my face.

"I'm not that hungry," I said.

"God, you don't eat. You always have your nose in a book. You've got to live a little," she said.

"Sorry," I said. I was always apologizing. I always have, ever since I was a kid. If I didn't catch a ball in gym class, I apologized. Even if someone was hurt in some way by someone else, I apologized. I had built-in guilt for all of the ails of the world, it seemed.

"Let's go," she said. " 'Days' is on in like five minutes. Come on Fido, I mean Nurse McKinley, the stories are starting."

"Don't call me Fido Miss Greenberg, I am not in the mood for your insolence," Nurse McKinley said.

Nurse McKinley was the only other nurse in the whole place who also wore a uniform. I don't know why Valerie hated her, she was nice to me. Although I could see if you were just out of school and still in that "question authority" phase how McKinley might get on your nerves. My perspective on a lot of that has changed since I had children. I am a lot more accepting of people's roles in the world. But not Valerie, and I had to admit it was fun to watch her harass McKinley. I missed that about myself sometimes. I missed my smart-ass days in high school when I would give a teacher a bunch of shit for no reason and feel absolutely no remorse.

"Oooh, big words," Valerie said. "Do they pay you extra to use words like that?"

"Just get in line," McKinley said. "If you want to get there faster, you'll help clean up this other table."

I went over and started picking up the trash on our section's other tables. Small tasks like cleaning and picking up after people didn't bother me now nearly as much as they used to. At home, I hated all of the tasks of housewifery. I got so sick of doing dishes all of the time, the constant pile of laundry, the constant mopping and wiping down of everything in site. It seemed never ending and pointless. Why do it - there will just be more tomorrow? But there, I don't know, I just didn't mind. It gave me comfort somehow.

The time after lunch was spent devoted to soap operas and smoking. Days of Our Lives was the favorite. I hadn't watched soaps so much since high school, when I came home every day after school and watched them.

There was nothing else to do and so I sat, smoking the Camel Lights my husband had lovingly and understandingly brought me and watched as Marlena, Bo and Hope battled demons and the Lazarus Stefano DiMera, who seemed to have more lives than the proverbial cat. It was amazing to me how quickly I could pick up on the story lines and how involved I could become in these fake people's lives. Don't get me wrong, I wasn't going to write fan mail or anything, but it was intriguing both to watch the show and to watch as the rest of the crew became involved. I always thought soap operas were crap, and would never admit to watching them, particularly to my housewifely acquaintances. I'd sooner admit to spending an afternoon in front of Sesame Street or Blue's Clues, but these soap characters - they had problems. I loved to watch Rhonda scream at the TV, begging a sweet, young thang not to sleep with so and so because he impregnated her mother or whatever.

Fascinating. We know how to fix the ails of every soap character and yet Jerry Springer could have a month's worth of shows from the five people in this very room. But who wanted to deal with that when it was a better agony waiting to find out if Bo and Hope would reunite for the four thousandth time?

Sitting there, in the oversized couch with the worn, scratchy fabric, I smoked and followed each drag with a sip off my water bottle. I made the effort to not think. For once, I was going to live in the moment and this in moment I was desperate for a Diet Coke. Something with caffeine. But there was no caffeine allowed on the second floor. It could react with our meds - they said. I think they just didn't want a bunch of women already proven hormonally instable running around with caffeine jitters, and that's understandable, it just didn't make getting up in the morning any easier.

The TV is soothing. I wanted to just lie there and watch the images flicker in front of me. I didn't want to read or nap or write or think. Just watch life, someone else's life, pass me by. This is peace in a way. In a really depressing way, I guess, but I took what I could get.

My peace is interrupted, as it usually is, by screaming. Not yelling, but actual, primal screaming, like someone is being killed. Normally, I would bolt up and have a look, but I have no energy for that and so I pull myself up and peer over the back of the couch.

Sheila is on the floor, writhing and kicking, banging her head against the hard floor.

"I won't go," she screams, over and over. I have no idea where they are trying to take her.

"Leave me alone," she yells. I am afraid she's going to knock herself unconscious. I grab a pillow from the couch and with as much authority as I can muster in my stride, walk over and place the pillow beneath her head. Nurse McKinley looks petrified, although I'm not sure why. Isn't she supposed to know how to deal with this?

I bend over Sheila, still screaming and kicking and grab her hand.

"Sheila...Sheila look at me," I said in my calmest of voices. For some reason, I am not afraid. "Look at me. What is wrong? Where are they taking you?"

She stops kicking for a moment and stares at me, her eyes wide and full of sheer terror. She doesn't speak.

In a flash, I am pushed aside by two large men dressed in green scrubs who pick her up and set her down hard in a wheelchair, strapping her feet and hands down with thick Velcro straps. I had learned about those straps when I worked in a nursing home, but I had never seen them used before. Sheila is whisked down the hallway and we don't see her again for a week.

I am left kneeling on the floor, holding onto the pillow. Nurse McKinley walked over and pulled me up by the arm.

"You shouldn't have done that," she said. "Sheila is confused and you are not trained to help her."

"But she was banging her head, on the floor, someone had to do something," I said. This is the first time I feel any of my old, sarcastic self creeping back into my head.

"I did something," she replied. "I called the orderlies and they took her to her treatment. Now, please go back to what you were doing." She is not unkind when she says this, but something in her tone says she felt suddenly threatened.

"Yeah, fine. OK. Whatever," I said. I walked back to the couch and sat down, but I immediately got back up. I didn't feel like watching TV anymore. My peace had been disrupted, but not by Sheila.

I went back to my room, sat on my bed and looked around. How did I get here?

Valerie walked in. She never knocks.

"Is she still sleeping?" she asked, pointing to my roommate Janet. Janet was permanently tucked in her bed. She never left unless one of the nurses came in and physically took her out. They had to use a wheelchair just to get her to meals.

"That's all she does," I said. "She hardly eats. I heard the doctor telling Nurse McLaughlin that they might have to consider giving her an IV just to keep her hydrated. But she'd probably just rip it out."

Janet was a mystery. She was much older than the rest of us, 50 or so, and didn't seem to have any family. Or at least, none that cared that she was here. They brought her here after she scared some kids on a playground. She had been living under the slide. From what I heard, she threatened them for playing in her house. One of the nurses said she grabbed one of them.

I tried to keep her water bottle filled and if she wouldn't come down for dinner, sometimes I brought her something back. Nurse McLaughlin, Debbie, she said we could call her, didn't mind, but if Nurse McKinley caught me bringing food back up, she yelled that if Janet was hungry, she could walk down with the rest of us.

"Hey," Valerie said. "That was pretty cool what you did. You calmed Sheila right down."

"Oh, I don't know," I said.

"No really," she said. "How did you know what to do with her?"

"I didn't really do anything," I said. "She just acted like my son did when he was small, throwing tantrums. Sometimes I would just hold him tight until he calmed down and then we could talk about what was bothering him so much."

"Cool. Wanna smoke?"

"Yeah, alright," I said. We weren't supposed to smoke in our rooms, but somehow when Valerie was around all of the rules went out the window. I felt like I was in high school again, ditching a class or smoking in the locker room.

"When's your next session with Dr. Lesbo?" she asked.

"Um, later," I said. "Four o'clock maybe."

"I saw her this morning. She said I should stay for a while, that I needed to come to terms with my issues or some shit like that. I told her I'd think about it, but there is a concert in Chicago I'd like to go to in a week."

"Oh yeah, who?"

"Stones. Big comeback tour, but it's like they're always coming back isn't it? My boyfriend said he got tickets off this guy he does some work for."

"That sounds fun. What kind of work does he do?

"Who?"

"You're boyfriend."

"Oh, yeah. Body work mostly. He doesn't work a lot, mostly he just hangs out in his dad's barn and fixes pieces of shit cars, but sometimes he gets paid."

"Kind of a freelancer, huh?"

"Yeah. A freelance auto body specialist. I'll tell him that the next time he comes, he'll think that's cool."

We sat there for a while, smoking silently, watching the smoke ring around the room. Nurse McKinley knocked once and walked in. I hastily put my cigarette out, but Valerie kept on smoking, watching her watching us.

McKinley fanned her face and pursed her nose and lips, but didn't say anything.

"Your doctor is ready for you now," she said, pointing at me.

I didn't like walking down the hall with McKinley. She smelled like vegetable soup and it reminded me of walking down the hall in my elementary school, usually behind a teacher determined to have the principal call my mother. I wasn't bad, exactly, in school. But I was loud and curious and bossy. I usually had an acceptable teacher every other year. A teacher who encouraged my questions and let me speak my mind. Those off years were the toughest. I would go back to school, excited to be alive and full of goals for a new year, and within days my enthusiasm would be squashed by a teacher who only wanted her students to be quiet and finish their assignments.

Valerie talked a lot about getting out, which was odd considering she was there voluntarily. She assembled us in my room - not her own, no one had ever been in Valerie's room - and stood in front of us and ranted about "banding together" and screwing the "motherfuckers." It was impressive stuff.

"You can't fight them," she said. "You have to not fight in order to beat them."

I knew what she meant, but I didn't help her explain it to the others. I sat back and watched as she went through her demonstration.

"You have to look right at them," she said. "You can't look like you think you know more than them and you can't look like you're sad. You have to be grateful...and remorseful."

"What's remorseful?" Rhonda asked.

"You have to look like you are sorry for trying to kill yourself," Sheila said.

"I didn't try and kill myself," Rhonda said. "I tried to kill my boyfriend." Then she burst out laughing. Rhonda was a tall black woman. She wasn't fat, but she was large and when she laughed, her breasts bounced like they were laughing along with her. A couple of the other girls joined her.

"Why would anyone want to kill themselves when they knows it's the men who cause all the trouble?"

Everyone laughed at Rhonda's stark admission. I pictured the women in the PTA back home in Onion Bay, a not so little harbor side New England-esque town on Lake Michigan, and wondered if they would have laughed as heartily. The Stepford Wives, my friend Emily and I called them. The wives of professors and doctors whose casual clothes were tidier and certainly more expensive than the clothes Em and I wore for going out.

I could have used Valerie's advice then, when I had countless Pampered Chef and Partylite Candle home parties to go to. I dreaded those events, but always accepted the invitation to go to one, thinking it would be a good way to have some fun and get out of the house. But they weren't. Who on earth decided that this was a good way to make money? These parties, Emily and I mused, were certainly rooted in the mafia. An underground coalition of upper middle-class wives whose sole purpose was to chisel money out of the lower middle-class masses. If the real mob only employed these women, surely breaking legs would become unnecessary as all that would be needed to get money from the debtor was a great catalog and good dose of guilt.

I had, though, perfected the art of being so overwhelmed by all of the things I wanted to buy that I must take the catalog home and then I would conveniently forget the date the order was due…until it was too late and the order was closed. "Oh, sugar," I said. "I missed my chance to spend $20 on a set of votive candles I could buy at Wal-Mart for $2.99. Silly me."

Valerie's advice would have been just as appropriate for the Stepford Wives as for the therapists, but I didn't know that then. I wanted to be one of them.

Is it wrong that I felt more comfortable there, among the lost and the angry? More and more, I dreaded going back, so Valerie's advice was of no use to me. I missed my children, of course, but everything else on the outside of this massive gray building frightened me. I wanted to be one of them - the normal. But as I sat in there among the Rhondas, Janets, Sheilas and even Valeries, it was quite evident that I had never been one of them and most likely, never would be, even if they did let me one day.

Them - with their perfectly coiffed, sporty-short haircuts and tastefully applied make-up, to make childrearing stylish, yet functional. Them - with their beautifully large, redecorated houses and a Merry Maid to clean it three times a week.

Me - my dark red, unruly, impossibly long and permanently frizzed hair in perfect concert with my cluttered, Goodwill and garage sale styles. I masked the embarrassment of my $3 green couch with comments on the value of frugality.

"I will recover it, of course," I said, "with a beautiful slipcover I found online."

Everyone applauded my brilliance. There was no slipcover and there was no $200 to pay for one even if I had found it. This I knew, but for a brief moment, as I served tea in mismatched teacups from the Salvation Army I called a collection, I belonged.

When I walked through the park and past the posher homes of our not quite downtown neighborhood, I felt like I belonged. People waved to me and the children. We went to the library and the little grocery store, all within walking distance of our small, cottage-like home. Wisconsin in the spring is really quite beautiful - once the mud dries. Trees fragrant with cherry and apple blossoms, their fallen petals like snow. My son Jack scooping them up by the handfuls and throwing them at a dog chained in a yard as I constantly snagged Madeline's stroller on bumps in the ragged sidewalk.

I grew up on a dairy farm in the center of the state, a place known for tornadoes that never felt the need to rip our farm apart. Although we were fortunate weather-wise, the same could not be said for the state of my family's finances. We were never rich, but my last two years in high school were the worst. We only had 100 cows, nothing like the new corporate farms coming into the area and eventually they won out. My parents sold the farm when I graduated from high school and moved to Madison, my father becoming a lobbyist for small farmers. I didn't miss the farm much when I graduated. I couldn't wait to get away from it and the constant stink of the cows, but that was then.

I've never been a joiner, which is probably why I was so silent in group sessions at the, the what? Hospital? Institution? Loony bin? Hospital, I guess. I was a lonely housewife, admittedly of my own volition. I certainly didn't blame Michael. He worked hard as an environmental scientist, always testing the waters in the bay or arranging public information meetings. He rearranged his schedule often so he could have three-day weekends with us, working 12-hour days the other four days of the week. And it's not that I was bored - I certainly had plenty to do, just lonely.

So, I tried Gymboree classes for the kids and playtimes at the Y, but felt hopelessly out of place among the overzealous mothers who constantly compared their children as if they were show ponies.

"My Sam took his first steps at 9 months," or "My Delilah's bowel movement was the best her doctor had ever seen." OK, I never actually heard the last one, but I might as well have for all the stimulating conversation these women had. Besides, how many times can you sing "This Old Man," before you give yourself a permanent hearing disability?

It wasn't until Jack went to kindergarten that I felt I finally found my place. With Madeline, then three, permanently attached to my leg, we volunteered at the school at least twice a week. We went on all of the class trips and attended every school function from Spring Fling to Book Fair.

It was this life I missed being in the hospital, but it wasn't that life that I left behind.

"Carrie?" Dr. Leslie asked.

"Hmmm?" I said.

"Are you ready to begin?"

I had no idea how long I had been sitting there, waiting for her, with the guard nurse watching me from outside the door. Had I fallen asleep? Maybe. Sometimes I couldn't tell where my daydreams ended and my sleep began.

"Yes, fine," I said. I did not exude the confidence in my therapy that Valerie said would get me out, but I tried to be, at the very least, complacent. I didn't have to try.

"So, how are things? The nurses tell me you've settled into your group activities."

"Yes."

"So, that's good, then. Has your family been to visit recently?"

"My husband comes every week."

"And the children?"

"Not as often - twice in the last month. His mother doesn't think it's good for them to come every week."

"Are they easily upset?"

"No. They understand as much as they can, I think. I think they pester his mother about when I'm coming back and she'd rather not talk about it all of the time."

"I see. Does that bother you?"

"That my mother-in-law's trying to replace me?"

"Is that what you think she's trying to do?"

"No. It's what she is doing. But it's not like I can blame her. I obviously can't handle the job."

"You're not here, Carrie, because you did anything to your children."

"Sure, technically."

"Why do you say that?"

"I don't know."

"I think you do."

"Well, I don't, so why don't you tell me? Isn't that, like, your job?"

I relished the sound of my sarcasm creeping back into my voice. It was ages since I had the nerve - or desire - to talk back and not care if there were consequences.

"No, Carrie, my job is to help you understand why you're here and then help you solve it."

"I see."

"Why am I here again, if I'm such a good mother?"

"You know why."

"Do good mothers try and kill themselves?"

"Sometimes."

Chapter 2

Night. I missed the dark. There was no dark at the hospital. There were patches of it, sure, and if you tried hard enough you could capture a patch for yourself. A patch under a pillow or a blanket, but the door was always ajar letting in that hideous fluorescent light from the nurses station and Janet kept her bedside light on all night. I thought it wouldn't bother me. After all, I slept with the lights on for years when the children were babies. They slept in a bassinet at the foot of my bed and I left the light in the closet on so that when they woke up for a nighttime feed or diaper change, I could go to them without waking up Michael or without tripping over the diaper bag or a basket full of unfolded laundry.

There, in my bed, I longed for darkness. I longed for an escape from the madness that surrounded me, engulfed me, and swirled like the whirling dervish in folktales through my head. It was quiet, for now. The only noise the plod of nurses trying to be quiet on their squeaky, sneakered feet. But I could hear them, whispering. Talking straight out sometimes. About us...them. Stories of children in school, teeth lost, boyfriends hated and then treasured again. Christmas gifts, Valentines, the nights an intoxicated jumble and me laying there, wishing for it to go away, but not too fast.

Gandhi was a Libra

A scream pierces the night. Who is it this time? I won't know until morning when the offender is missing from breakfast. The chairs scraped across the floor as the night staff took their positions. Will security be needed? Are restraints in order? Usually. They scramble through cabinets for the right drug to subdue, a call to the doctor, apologetically, asking for permission. The screaming continues.

And then silence. I was sleepy, but often could not sleep until the sun started to peer through the window shades and then sleep came deeply. Until that point, I could entertain myself, often with the images of my dancing children, playing on a beach or in the yard, but when that became finally too painful for me to bear, I thought of death. Of suicide. Of the multitude of ways to do it. I had cured myself of a fear of heights by imagining the final plunge off a building. I could feel myself standing on the edge, arms spread wide, and a tumble to the pavement below. Would I see the sky or the earth as I fell to the ground? Would I regret it and beg God to forgive me in that final second? Would I black out from the fear of the fall? Scare myself to death before my insides were shattered?

Another night might bring an image of a car, not my car, but an anonymous car, driven by me into a lake, sinking slowly. Death by drowning would never be my first choice and so I feared that when I did die, that would be how I would go.

Driving in a car, always alone, never with the children, I often had to fight the impulse not to drive head on into a passing tractor-trailer. The temptation was too real, too finite, too easily excused. An accident, one most certain to end my life, but I could never do it - make that final cross into the other lane, my mind too rigid on the rules of driving.

And always I would think of the person who would find me, laying on the pavement or the tractor-trailer driver who hit me. What a terrible thing to have to remember, to be a part of, even if the dead person wanted it to happen.

I knew my husband would be the one to find me that day. I knew it because I planned it that way. I drove the children to my mother's house for the weekend, wrote the letters, notarized the will. I laid myself on the floor in the spare room so that he wouldn't have to remember seeing me that way in our bed, or on our couch. I put the pills, 50 of them I counted out, in front of me on the floor and then swallowed them, quickly, five at a time. Each time I took a swig of the vodka I bought for my last birthday party, crying, praying for a God I don't believe in to forgive me and have pity on my children. To give them a good life. I knew what I was doing. I meant it with all of my heart. I didn't mean to come back.

But I did and now I dream of suicide because once your mind gets to that place where you can dream about it, you can't go back. I once heard an alcoholic describe people who drink socially. He couldn't imagine how a person could leave half a glass of wine at a table, or drink only one drink at a party. How could you not want the whole bottle? What was the point if you didn't get drunk?

I felt that way about suicide sometimes. How could you not think about it? It becomes such an easy, comforting road to go down? Screw up and, no worries, just kill yourself. Didn't everyone feel that way?

"No, everyone does not feel that way," Valerie said one afternoon in the day room. "There's too much to do and too short a time to do it in. Who cares if you screw up? You'll screw up again."

This made too much sense to come from one of us. Valerie's sense of self, her complete confidence in her thoughts and actions, confused me. Not because she possessed them, but because she was here. She made sense and yet, she was here.

Valerie did not talk about her past. She talked about the future. She talked about getting out and all of the things she would do when she did. She talked about escaping. Since she had no need to escape, it sounded like that was her own dream. She constantly referred to rock music as poetry, peppering her daily rants with lyrics from Nirvana and other bands I had heard of but never listened to, because the development of my album inventory stopped sometime in the early 1980s with the purchase of a Wham! record (yes, vinyl). Jack, Maddie and I frequently cleaned the house to the Beatles or Jimmy Buffet's Margaritaville. Billy Joel was also a favorite among those under five.

But Valerie Greenburg interested me. Her name sounded more like one of the Stepford Wives I had escaped than the ranting rebel I came to know. From her baggy scrub bottoms and baggy hooded sweatshirts (drawstrings removed) to her streaky blonde hair, she oozed attitude and sex. One couldn't help but be attracted to her - no matter your sexual orientation - which for most in there was iffy at best.

This hospital bred bisexuals. Women who hated the men they left behind, yet hooted and hollered like construction workers at every sexy (or not) janitor, security guard or CNA that moved through our halls.

Valerie attracted them all, men and women alike. The women clustered around her, begged to rub her back or hold her hand on the way to dinner. And she obliged them enough to keep them coming back for more, but was not afraid to say not only "no," but "Get the fuck away from me" without incurring anyone's wrath.

I was attracted to Valerie too, but not in a sexual way. Not that I was above fantasizing about women, far from it. I found myself often in bed thinking of beautiful women, but they were anonymous women, faceless. I never craved female companionship the way the women there did. Or any companionship for that matter. It was odd enough when I met Michael because I had never before desired to be around someone for long lengths of time. I liked being alone. Other people bored me and I hated having to hear the same sad stories over and over. Birthing stories and career stories and where I went to college stories. I spent inordinate amounts of time trying to look interested while simultaneously trying to think of something to say in return. With Michael it was different. We could be together and not have to talk and then just as easily pick up a conversation we had left two days ago without having to rehash the backstory. It was like that with Valerie too, I noticed.

Valerie had something extra. She seemed to genuinely enjoy listening to other people and trying to help them with her problems. I was never a leader. Valerie was born to the task.

I wanted to know her more and asked her flat out one day why she was in the hospital. The response was frightening.

"I'm a junkie, OK?" she screamed. "I take everything. Drink everything - is that what you want to know about me?"

I froze. She left, slamming my door and didn't speak to me for two days. But as shocking as her response was, I didn't buy it. I don't know why, but the outburst seemed made up. I didn't doubt that she had drug or alcohol problems, but that wasn't why she was here. It couldn't have been.

Chapter 3

We were as maximum security as you could get without being in maximum security. We were supervised, checked and rechecked. We were guided and dragged everywhere, and one fine day, Rick decided to take us out.

Getting ten relatively normal women ready to go out to the movies can take hours. It took most of the ten of us literally days to get ready for our evening out. Special requests from home for normal clothes had to be made, make-up had to be begged and borrowed from other floors - mostly from the old women on the ground floor nursing home who were not restricted in the types of luxury items they could have. Our only luxury items were cigarettes and books. And usually only a few of us had books. The old women would meet us in the courtyard during our recess (we had reverted to using schoolyard terms for our daily routines) and would sneak us compacts full of bright eyeshadows and blushes. They were just as excited as we were, but for them the excitement lied in the sneaking around, talking to the dangerous girls from floor two, and getting cigarettes or a Playgirl magazine in return.

I watched as Valerie helped one woman take off her oxygen mask, just so she could have a drag off of Valerie's Marlboros. I almost intervened, but the smile on the old woman's face kept me at bay.

All of this was done under the ignoring gaze of Nurse McLaughlin, McKinley would never have allowed it.

The Saturday afternoon of our impending departure found me in my room, trying to do something with the hair now too short to do anything with, but I was alone, not willing to participate in the madness outside my door. The shrieks of delight from the girls who were trading clothes and sharing the contraband make-up were too much to bear. I was just not that excited about going out, but I never was. I was not one of those wives who begged her husband to take her out on Saturday night. Whether this was because of ingrained financial circumstances or my preference for an old movie on TV or a book, I am not certain. I liked taking the children out and any spare cash I had was spent going to zoos or museums or even the local pizza place with Maddie and Jack.

But, as reluctant as I was to go out, there was something irresistible about the prospect of not only being out of the hospital and seeing the world again, but the looks on people's faces as they watched women from the crazy house invade their normalcy. That was something I could not miss for the world. So, I put on my jeans and the nice sweater Michael brought me the weekend before and waited at a table in the TV room until Rick came to get us and the girls were ready.

"Alright, ladies," Rick said when we were properly assembled, "let's go."

Rick had also called in a few favors and gotten several CNAs to go along with us, his optimism and enthusiasm for the trip no doubt hampered by the thought of someone escaping - or worse, causing a scene.

The girls giggled in the van, fawning over Valerie and begging her to sit by them at the theater. I was reminded of high school once again, the girls always surrounding the popular ones, begging to belong. Was I ever one of them? Certainly not a popular girl, but a groupie? I hoped not. I think I tried once, maybe in fifth grade, to belong like that. I remember the girl, too. A little taller than the rest of us, hair blonde and a little longer than ours. She was the one allowed to wear dangling earrings, shoes with heals and make-up before the rest of us. She stayed up late on school nights, or, at least, she told us she did. And there were others like her, maybe not as tall or blonde, but with heeled shoes and dangling earrings. Or maybe they were tall and blonde, but still wore their tomboyish jeans and baseball shirts. I was none of these, of course.

My red hair made me the fodder for much teasing - mostly by the boys. The girls would never say anything out loud, but would whisper among themselves at lunch, glancing over once in a while, just enough to let me know they were talking about me. My clothes were not that much different, and while my earrings didn't hang an inch from my ear, they were pretty and grown up looking. I had long since given up the frilly barrettes my mother used to pull back my unruly hair, but still, I did not belong. I also don't know why it mattered so much. I seem to be more hurt now remembering it, than I was at the time. I had friends. Some of them were goofy like me, most of them were boys, but they were friends. And occasionally, on a rainy Saturday afternoon, one of the "cool" girls who lived down the street would invite me over. Better to have someone over than no one, I'm sure. For all of my fear and loathing of the way they treated me, I always went, hopeful that this would be the time when I would become something better than I was, but Monday morning always came and it was always the same. Lunch with the boys who four square, not football.

And the same was true through high school. Why would anything have changed? I was popular only in a very superficial sense. No one hated me, I was not the object of ridicule any longer, because I had proven myself to be smart and outgoing. But while I always had someone to go to a dance with, I was never invited to those after hours parties where the gossip took place. I don't know that I would have gone, even if I had been invited.

High school soon brought me, however, to another place where I exceeded even the most popular of girls. Sex. My willingness to have sex brought me the affection I craved and got me through, along with my books, the long, dreary days until graduation - although just barely.

Of course, I had been taught all of the things about sex that a girl should know. We weren't comfortable talking about it, my mother and I, but it wasn't banished conversation. I know if I had had questions, I could have asked. I just simply preferred to find the answers out on my own. So, I participated in extra-curricular activities and on the long bus rides home, I let the boy who liked me at that moment feel under my shirt or put his tongue in my mouth. I did not mind it and I looked forward to this one rebellious streak in me being found out by the next boy. I did not smoke, drink or do any drugs. Sex was my drug and I loved it. And I loved being loved…or as close to it as I could get.

The girls fawning over Valerie brought it back, all of it, including the one night my sexuality backfired.

Despite my willingness to do almost anything, I had not done "it" yet. I often considered going all the way with a boy, but something held me back. Maybe it was Nancy Reagan and the "Just Say No" to drugs campaign ringing in my head, or maybe it was just plain fear, but I couldn't do it, not yet. And then one day, I decided I could.

After school on an early spring day, Corey Evans took my hand and with the promise of something more ringing in his head, led me to his mother's classroom, she was a teacher, in the deserted school and into a closet with carpeting on the floor. I thought I was ready, but once his hand probed too deeply between my legs, I realized I couldn't do it, not like that. Besides I was terrified of a janitor walking in on us. I didn't love Corey, but I didn't hate him either. We were friends. We hung out in the parking lot after school and worked on the school paper together - he, the writer and me, the photographer. It was comfortable and silly as we kissed and took of each other's shirts. But it got serious, fast and I didn't want to be a tease, but I didn't want to keep going. He poked and prodded beneath my underwear and it stopped feeling good. The wetness that had been pouring out of me was slowing to nothing, but was still there.

I could see him, face red, ready, not willing to stop. I pushed his hands away and tried to be light about it. Let's wait until we can go somewhere nicer, I said. Come, on, cut it out. I have to go. No way, he said. You said we could. I pushed him off and without warning, the back of his hand hit my jaw. I was stunned. No one, not even my parents, had hit me in the face before. I laid back on the floor and cried and Corey still did not stop, pulling my jeans just far enough down, my legs just wide enough to find the leftover wetness that was there. His face came down to mine and he kissed me, hard, pushing into me, telling me what a bitch I was the whole time. A tease. And isn't this what I wanted? Tears streamed down my face. I waited, my head banging a box of books, until the ramming was done. The piercing pain of him driving into my stomach. I thought about a homework assignment I had to do.

I sat up, the wetness, his wetness pouring out of me. No one told me that when sex was over you'd need a towel. I pulled up my jeans and put my hair in a ponytail. That wasn't so bad, now was it? He held out his hand to pull me up and I took it. He kissed me on the neck. Next time will be better, he said. You'll see.

I was startled awake from my horrid walk down memory lane by Valerie's face peering into mine. She came up from behind me and put her lanky arms, still tanned from wherever she was before around my neck, much like my son does when I am sitting at the kitchen table drinking my morning coffee.

"Whatcha thinking about?" she asked.

"Oh, nothing much. Kids, that kind of thing," I said.

"Do ya miss 'em?"

"Yeah, a lot. But I guess I'm glad I'm not there anymore too."

"I never saw the deal about kids, I mean, why does everyone think they're so great? All they do is make messes and whine and cry all the time."

"Yeah, that's true," I said. "They do make an awful mess, but it's worth it, I guess, because they are so much fun. I just like to do things with them - and for them."

"So why are you glad you're here? With us? Didn't they make you crazy?"

"I don't think it was the kids who made me crazy...I think it was everything else."

"Yeah."

"Anyway," I said, trying to make my voice lighter, "what movie are we going to see?"

"Something light," Rick said from the front of the van. "A comedy...definitely."

"Nothing too dramatic for the girls from crazy," Valerie said and the van began to rock with laughter. Rhonda, Sheila, who just came back from solitary not three days before the outing, and even Janet, persuaded to come along, made crazy faces and started yelling that they were at a strip bar.

"Girls, girls," Rick said, trying to sound authoritative. "Let's just relax, please, we're almost there."

The van pulled up to the curb of the theater and we all stumbled out, stepping on each other's shoes, like the clown car packed full in the circus. I hadn't noticed until then just how disturbed we looked. The girls, all ten of them, full grown women all, were a mismatched set of sweatpants and leather pants and jeans and blue eye shadow and bright red and pink lipstick. Hair was teased and sprayed until it practically stood on end and all of them, every last one, thought they looked good - checking themselves in a window before getting their tickets.

What would the Stepford Wives say if they could see me? Surely they would be happy I was put in my place. Certainly, I would rather be there with

Valerie, Rhonda, Sheila, even Janet, than any of them. I glanced around at the other theater patrons, straightened my cable knit sweater and proudly walked among the group, following Rick, whom I also noticed was glancing around a little, wondering if he knew anyone. At least he could say he was doing his job.

I continued to walk proudly and smiled with them as they pawed the glass display cases bursting with treats. We were limited to popcorn and Sprite, of course, a little sugar, but no caffeine to speak of. My association with Valerie had suddenly boosted me up in the ranks and soon I was having seats saved for me all over the theater. Rick took control and made us sit together, cowed by a fear of losing us, and I sat next to him, wondering if he hoped no one he knew would see us together.

Our movie was appropriate for all ages and so the frequent calls of "Mommy," or the crying of a toddler repeatedly tugged at me. I wanted to go the children and I felt guilty for not being with my own. It was not unlike the feeling I had when I took on a weekend job waiting tables in a diner and the parents would bring their little angels out to breakfast and I would wait on them, fawning over the children, wishing I could fawn over my own. Then, of course, I would be too tired once I got home to do much fawning at all, making me feel even worse about my parenting skills.

I got through the terrible movie somehow. I wish I could remember the plot, but I don't think there was one.

Once the theater lights came up, I was ready for bed, but there was still pizza to be had and we made a terrible noise walking down the street to the restaurant. It seemed that Rick and I were the only ones who cared if people recognized us, but then I realized that everyone else was from somewhere else. Only I had lived in this town before going to the hospital.

We entered the restaurant I had been to a thousand times before with my family. A nice, low-key place where kids could write on a chalkboard wall while the parents waited for the food to arrive and tried to think of something interesting to talk about besides school and the children's disciplinary issues.

Michelle Kennedy

And, of course, it happened. A Stepford Wife, wiping down her child's sauce-covered mouth as we walked in the door. All of my confidence flooded out and my heart pounded in my chest. I found a booth and slunk into it, hoping to God she wouldn't see me. But it was impossible not to notice us as the rest of the girls pulled tables together, making them screech across the floor and borrowing chairs from other tables. Rick climbed in next to me.

"What's up?"

"Um…nothing," I said, trying to keep the shivering out of my voice.

"Uh, huh…"

"No, it's just, someone I know is here," I said.

"A friend?"

"Not exactly, at least, not anymore."

"I see, well, just be cool. If they notice you, just be polite and let it go."

But I wouldn't let it go, I knew I wouldn't. If she talked to me I would cry. I was starting to cry already. I could feel it, the tears in my eyes already beginning to form, the lump hardening with each breath in my throat.

"Carrie? Is that you?" It was Franny Schmidt. Her husband was a dentist and she lived in the biggest house on Main Street. She sent her little one to the counter to pay the check with her father.

"Um…hi," I said. I didn't want to over do it…I tried to remain calm.

"Oh, my dear, are you out on the town?" she said. Then she lowered her voice to a whisper, "they let you do that?"

Why was she being nice to me? I didn't want her to be nice to me. I wanted her to just give me a dirty look and go away.

"Yeah."

"We went to a movie," Sheila said, just like Jack would have. "And now we're having pizza!"

"Yes, I can see that," she nodded and smiled to Sheila like she would to a small child. Her charity work for the day is done. "Well, it is just so good to see you are doing so well. I saw your little Jack just the other day - my he's a smart boy."

It was clear now, she wasn't being nice. She was sticking the dagger in slowly, twisting it jaggedly as it went in. She saw more of my Jackie than I did.

"Yes, he is."

"Well, looks like the gang is ready to go," she said. Then she looked me in the eyes, her intense gaze as sharp as the dagger, and put one hand down on our table as if to make sure this point was perfectly clear. "You, take care of yourself."

Needless to say, I didn't eat. I spent the rest of our time at the restaurant with my head turned to the wall, listening to the girls pick on cute waiters and eat mounds of pizza. On the way home, I imagined the leap off every building we passed. Would that one be high enough?

Chapter 4

S o you take pictures?" Dr. Leslie said during our next session. She
varied her bright, hippy, yet somehow exceedingly predictable
wardrobe on this day with a hat. A skull cap of what looked to be
Guatamalan descent with her long salt and pepper braid wagging along her
broad back as she moved papers from one pile of clutter to the other.

"I did," I said. It is true, I was a photographer before I went crazy.

"Well, that's just wonderful. What a great job. Do you miss it?"

"Not so much." And it's true. I hadn't missed it at all since I had been in
here. When I did think about it, I spent more time considering how odd it was
that I didn't miss it, rather than thinking about actually taking pictures.

"Tell me about it. How did you get interested in photography?"

"I liked taking pictures and it seemed to be as good a job as any." That
was mostly true. Before I had children, I traveled all over the state taking
portraits. I liked photographing old people… people who had lived seemingly
unassuming lives, but when you took the picture, you could see more. You
could see that they had lived life fully whether through joy or fear or sheer
survival.

My photo career, if you can call it that, began with one photo, taken
when I was 15. I had previously taken my father's Canon AE-1 as my own and
walked around the small Wisconsin town I grew up in, taking pictures of

everything. My father helped me set up a dark room in the basement bathroom and, with the help of my high school art teacher, I learned how to develop my own film. I loved sitting in that room, alone, quiet, tipping the canister of chemicals back and forth slowly. I loved enlarging the images and watching them become something I had seen.

The picture of consequence was one I took on a whim. A portrait of a lady, maybe 70 years old, taking the sign down from her bookshop. The bookshop was a destination in my town, but when a larger bookstore opened in the new strip mall, she was unable to keep it open. It wasn't a unique story by any means. Plenty of shops downtown were going out of business because of new K-Marts or SuperSaves going up around us. But something about the sadness in this woman's eyes caught me and I took the shot. A couple of days later, I gave this picture to my art teacher and she sent it in to the St. Elizabeth Daily Dispatch, a paper that's name expected more of it than the publication itself could give.

I didn't know anything of it until it appeared the following day, complete with my name under the photo. I was hooked. I never imagined at that point that I could do anything with the photos that were cluttering up boxes in my mother's basement. Suddenly, I felt validated, only I didn't know that then. When the check for $10 arrived a week later, an even better indicator of my worth, I decided to submit pictures to the paper all of the time. I was hired part-time after school and was the photographer on call when a tornado ripped our wee town apart. A picture I took of someone's still trailered speed boat in the entryway of the local hotel made the wire service and was printed in papers all over the country. I was convinced I had arrived.

I skipped out on college in favor of full-time position at the paper. My parents had left for Madison, and although they were only an hour away, I chose to stay in St. Elizabeth, renting a studio apartment above the bakery. I learned more about photography from the photo editor, Bill Thomas, than I learned in any of the courses I occasionally took at the local technical college.

I read everything I could get my hands on about taking pictures. I subscribed to every magazine and followed him relentlessly on shoots. Because I worked for a small paper, I was given the opportunity to shoot everything, from portraits of local business leaders to stills for the advertisers. I learned about lighting and F-stops and bracketing my shots. I carried a reflector around in my beat up old Toyota Corolla so if I had to take outside shots I could generally ensure good light. We never took color photos for the paper. It wasn't like it is now, with all of the digital equipment and photo retouching on the computer. If the lighting wasn't good or if you messed up the shot, there was no fixing it later back at the office. The shot had to be good, clear, and exposed properly and if it wasn't, you lost your space to a photographer who had done it right. I received several angry glares from reporters who needed photos with their stories but didn't get them because I had messed up the picture. I made plenty of mistakes, but rarely the same one twice.

Before long, I was referred by Bill to take pictures for local calendars put out by the St. Elizabeth Chamber of Commerce and my old art teacher framed some of my photos and put them on display in the bank and the library.

I met Michael at a journalism conference at the university in Madison. He was a lecturer on covering the environment and I was trying to give the Daily Dispatch their money's worth by taking every seminar I could. I had promised Bill that I would take seminars for both photography and reporting and give a "talk" when I got back.

I distinctly remember walking into the auditorium and sitting down near a door so I could escape easily in case it was unbearably boring. But as soon as Michael walked in, I couldn't breathe, much less think of escaping. He was simply beautiful and I couldn't take my eyes off him, although I couldn't hear a word he said. I tried to concentrate so that I could ask him a question at the end of his lecture that would sound reasonably intelligent, but I couldn't think of one. I left at the end of the lecture completely taken and positive I'd never see him again because I was such a dope.

I walked to the nearest canteen, ordered a cup of coffee and looked down embarrassed at my notebook, upon which I had written absolutely nothing except the date and doodled some ivy leaves, the only thing I can draw. My hands were still shaking and I looked up every time I heard a door close, hoping it was him. I had no plan if I actually saw him, but just wanted a glimpse.

You're insane, I told myself. You never get the truly beautiful guys, you always get their good friends. I was actually contemplating trying to find out who his friends were just so I could see him occasionally when he appeared at my table.

"Hi," he said. "You were in my last seminar, right?"

Stunned and nearly speechless I mumbled, "Mmm hmm."

"Do you mind if I sit here?" he asked. "This place is packed and I don't know anyone."

"Yeah, sure," I said. "Please do."

"So, you didn't escape from your seat by the door," he said. "Does that mean I wasn't completely boring?"

I laughed.

"No, not completely," I said. And then he grabbed my notebook. Shit, I thought. I tried to grab it back, but he flipped to the first page, where there was nothing.

"Wow, I so completely enthralled you that you couldn't even take notes," he said. His smile was broad and I could tell that there was no anger in his eyes. So I laughed again.

"Completely enthralled," I said. And then I swear I blushed. I could feel the heat rushing my face and ears.

"Oh well, the reporting of geological surveys and coastal erosion doesn't enthrall everyone the way it does me."

"Indeed," I said. "How could it not?"

And that was it. We were inseparable from then on. He finished his Ph.D. at Madison and I went home to St. Elizabeth, but I started visiting my parents every weekend just so I could be with him, and he drove the hour to St. Elizabeth every evening he could just to be with me. We were married when he finished his degree a year later and moved to Onion Bay on the coast of Lake Michigan. I was 20, he was 25 and everything I could have ever wanted in a guy. I had to leave my job at the paper, but I didn't care. I was in love and suddenly, very much, wanted to be his wife.

It all seemed so long ago. But it wasn't, really. Just five short years and I had done a lifetime's worth of damage in them.

"Do you have your camera here?" Dr. Leslie asked.

"No."

"I think you should ask your husband to bring it for you."

"No. What could I possibly take pictures of here?"

"I'll bet you'd be surprised."

"I doubt it." She was starting to grate on my nerves. Why couldn't she just let the whole photography thing go? I did it. I don't do it anymore. What's wrong with that? People change careers all of the time.

"Yes, that's true," she said.

"What's true," I said.

"That people change careers all the time."

"I said that out loud?"

"Yes. So, do you see this as some sort of career change?"

"No, I mean…that's not what I meant."

"Then what did you mean?"

"Let's just say that I no longer have the desire to take pictures, OK? Can we just leave it at that?"

"Today we will," she said. "But you'll need to face up to it eventually, you know. What happened had nothing to do with your pictures. I've seen your pictures, they're quite good." She flipped through my file, and then paused on something as if it was very interesting.

"You're a Libra," she said. "Did you know Gandhi was a Libra?"

"So?"

"Don't you think that's interesting?"

"Why?"

"Hmm. Not sure. What do you know about Gandhi?"

"Not much. Can I please go now?" The patchouli, cat piss-laden air was too much. I was going to throw up. I didn't want to think about this. Not right now. Not yet. I wanted to go back to bed. I wanted it to go away.

"Yes, you can go." I got up quickly and went to the door where a new nurse was waiting to escort me back to the floor.

"But Carrie," she said. "It won't go away until you put it away."

The walk back to the floor was interminable. The new nurse was chatty. Telling me about her new boyfriend and how much she loved nursing. I nodded and smiled weakly. When we walked through the doors, both of them, one set of double doors that she needed her ID to enter, letting them lock behind us and then another set of doors she had an access code to enter, Valerie was right behind them. She jumped out and mauled me. She hung on my back, pushing me on to the smoke room.

"I don't feel like smoking," I said.

"Sure you do, besides I'm out of smokes, I have to bum yours."

"Alright." I was too tired to argue. We opened the smoke room door and although a nasty haze hung at the ceiling, it was empty, unusual for the middle of the day.

"Where is everyone?" I asked.

"Outside, doing trust training or some shit with Rick."

"Why aren't you out there?"

"I wanted to wait for you."

"Why?"

"So we could snoop."

"Snoop?"

"Yeah. I need some Valium or something and I know not everyone in here is taking their pills. We're gonna find them." She took a last drag on her cigarette and stomped it into the linoleum.

"We're not alone up here, you know," I said. "There are at least two nurses up at the desk."

"I know, but they won't pay any attention to us. Come on. It'll be fun." And the truth was, it sounded like fun. Suddenly, I was pumped up and ready to go, the fatigue fading away.

"Alright," I said, jumping off the table I was sitting on. "Where do we start?"

"Megan's room. She never looks tired." Megan was one of the least interesting patients. She was about 25 and ostensibly in for alcoholism. She must have been arrested for disorderly conduct somewhere along the way. That was the way most rehab patients got in there. Because it was a county hospital, it did everything. If you didn't have money for one of the private rehab facilities, you went there. I suppose the county would have been pleased if anyone paid for the privilege, but that was rare. Occasionally, a well-dressed older man would get the walking tour of the floor with the hospital administrator. We would all be told to sit quietly and play cards or read. But we could see, as the administrator opened the doors, that this is not what the older man had in mind for his daughter or his wife or whoever he was sending there.

The smell would get him right away. We laughed as we watched him wriggle his nose then try and regain his composure, placing his nose a little higher in the air. On one such occasion, when a former mayor was walking through, we were told to sit up and smile at him, to let him know we were all happy as clams to be in there. Valerie, of course, agreed during the little meeting Nurse McKinley held the night before, but the next morning, she came ripping out of her room in a wheelchair hijacked from someone at breakfast.

She wheeled right up to the former mayor and winked at him, whispering to him to please get her out, that it was all a mistake. He bent down to hear her better, ever the concerned politician, and when Nurse McKinley tried to pull Valerie's chair away, Valerie latched onto the mayor's leg, falling out of the chair and screaming "Please…get me out of here! The treatments! They're too much! I can't take it anymore! It's inhuman!"

It took three nurses and a burly nursing assistant named Mike to get her off of him. She thrashed so hard she made blood come out of her nose. The rest of us, quietly playing cards, were stunned. I was still relatively new and was unsure how much of Valerie's act was really an act, until she winked at us.

"What on earth," the mayor said. "What is this poor girl in for?"

Nurse McKinley looked at the floor, as did the hospital administrator.

"I demand to know," he said.

"She's in rehab," McKinley said, knowing that this admission would be the last the hospital would see of the mayor. Valerie did a victory dance as the administrator and the mayor walked out of the doors, the mayor berating the poor Ms. Kelly and demanding reports of every kind.

Valerie's dance ended abruptly when McKinley had Mike take her to solitary. Solitary was the same type of room as the suicide watch rooms. The same floor mat and nothing else, but the door was kept closed, with only a small square window with which to peer at the offender.

As Mike approached her, Valerie began to kick and scream, much like she had in front of the mayor, but this time, her eyes were wild.

"No, no…Debbie, don't" she pleaded. "Please, I'm sorry…I'm sorry." Seeing Valerie frightened was not something many of us had witnessed. It was terrifying. McKinley took a syringe out of her pocket and placated Valerie enough so she could be dragged to isolation. She was there for a week. We caught glimpses of her when the door was opened to give her a bedpan or to give her another shot, but that was all.

She looked terrible. Her hair was matted and frayed and she sat against the wall, dazed and glassy-eyed. If there was one thing I could say about Valerie, it's that while the rest of us usually looked like we just got out of bed (which most of us did), Valerie always looked like a supermodel. She always took a shower first thing, did her hair and make up and even though we only had sweatshirts and scrub pants to wear, she wore them with style. She rolled the waistband down over her hips to reveal a tanned, smooth, flat belly, an anomaly on the floor and while we weren't allowed any jewelry, she had several marvelous tattoos. One of leaves and flowers around her wrist and a Celtic knot of some kind around her ankle.

I admired this tattoo again as she hiked up her pant legs and tiptoed down the corridor.

"I feel sneakier if we tiptoe," she said. We acted like spies as we rounded the hallway in front of the nurses' desk, running on tiptoes when their backs were turned to our destination.

In front of Megan's door, I noticed it was blank. Most of the girls covered their doors in posters or pictures cut out from the magazines in the TV room, but upon closer inspection - due to Valerie shoving me up against the door, face first, because a nursing assistant had glanced down the hallway - I noticed a tiny piece of paper, the length of a thumbnail. It was plastered underneath a piece of Scotch tape in the middle of the door and on it was one tiny typewritten word, "no," all in lowercase.

I nodded my head toward the paper and Valerie said, "Yeah, Megan's weird."

"Aren't we all?" I asked.

"Yeah." Valerie then raised her eyebrows and grinned wide as she snapped the door knob with one quick turn of the wrist and opened the door.

I stood there, at the entrance, dumbfounded by the filth within. Valerie grabbed my sleeve and yanked me in.

"Jesus, will you look at this place? If I kept my room like this McKinley would kill me," she said. Clothes covered the floor and it was impossible to tell the clean from the dirty.

"No kidding," I said. "Hey - Megan doesn't have a roommate either. What's up with that?"

"Megan is the daughter of a senator - straight from the boarding school," Valerie said. "Well, not exactly straight. She made a few pit stops along the way."

"What on earth would the daughter of a senator be doing here? Aren't there nicer places?"

"I think Daddy got a little fed up with his baby girl and hoped this place would shock her out of her wayward ways," Valerie said. "Oh, God...it stinks in here."

Valerie picked up a shirt or two off the floor and then tossed them across the room in disgust. She crossed the room without any regard for what she was stepping on and made her way to Megan's dresser. She pulled a box off her bookshelf and waved me over.

"Oh, ick," I yelled as I tried to avoid a pretty, yet oddly moldy looking dress, and stepped into a pizza box, half full of stale pizza. I turned my ankle as the box slipped beneath me and tried to jump away, but banged my knee into the dresser.

"Jesus," Valerie said. "You're gonna get everyone in here."

"Sorry," I whispered.

"Whatever. Are you alright?"

"Yeah," I said.

"Let's see what Daddy's little girl has in here," Valerie said, opening the makeup box.

"It's just makeup," I said. "Look."

"The top level is just makeup..." Valerie said.

Of course, she was right. Underneath was a stash of pills that would rival any doctor's wife's medicine cabinet.

"The one thing this girl keeps organized is her dope," Valerie said.

The pills were apparently organized by size and then I noticed, by color.

"Roy G. Biv," I said, out loud.

"What?" Valerie looked at me.

"Um...Roy G. Biv," I said pointing out each group of pills in turn. "Red, orange, yellow, green, blue, indigo, violet. The colors of the rainbow."

"Oh," Valerie said. "Is there anything you don't know?"

"Plenty..like, what the hell does she need all of those pills for? She obviously doesn't take them."

"Maybe she's Daddy's supplier!" Valerie laughed so hard she fell over on the bed. I couldn't help but laugh too, watching her was more than I could bear.

"So, is she really in here for rehab?" I asked.

"Partly, I think," Valerie said. "She shows up every few months, usually right after she gets an abortion."

"What?"

"Yeah, she's had like 10, and she's only 20 years old," Valerie said. "It's amazing she can still get pregnant."

"Jesus," I said. I immediately pictured Jack and Maddie back at home, playing the backyard, running around, giving me worms to look at.

"I know," Valerie said. "No one is supposed to know, of course, but I heard screaming one day when I was in solitary. Every one thinks those rooms are soundproof, but they're not. I learn more in there then anywhere else. Anyway, she was screaming at - it had to be McKinley - about loving some guy and fucking everyone to get out of her house. But, I don't know. How had could she have it? I mean, I grew up in a crappy apartment with my father and brothers. I was lucky to get dinner on my fucking birthday, so it's hard for me to feel sorry for her."

"Why so many abortions," I asked. "It sounds like her parents could have afforded to help her?"

"Yeah, they helped her…right to the abortion clinic and then into this room," Valerie said. "Can't have a senator with an unwed teenage mother on his hands."

"That's dumb…people don't think that way anymore, do they?"

"Some people must," Valerie said. "Anyway, what do you want out of here? I grabbed some Valium. This looks like Prozac and this is…"

The door flew open and Megan came screaming through it. What happened next is only a blur now, but I remember the pills flying and a scream, a piercing shriek unlike anything I had ever heard before. For a long time, I thought it was Megan's scream, but learned much later that it was my own.

The first tackle caught me at chest level and threw me against the headboard of her bed. I remember her face red and angry, her sweat dripping on me as she grabbed my neck and looked me in the eyes. Curiously, I don't remember any pain. There must have been some, but I can't remember feeling it. I do remember the feel of my Adam's Apple pressed against what felt like the back of my throat, to this day the thought makes me gag, and I can see Valerie out of the corner of my bulging eyes, first pulling on Megan, then grabbing a chair and hitting her with it.

The crack of the chair released me, I am told, and brought the staff running into the room. But I don't remember any of that. Just darkness as Valerie raised the chair above her head.

Chapter 5

Michael looked down at me like he used to and for a brief moment, I forgot it all - the hospital, Valerie, Megan - the reasons I was there to begin with,

"Hey, how're you feeling?" Michael ran his hand along my forehead and down my cheek.

I looked at him and then the white room around us. I looked up at the I.V. pole and the tube that ran down into my hand.

"My head hurts," I whispered and smiled weakly and tried to touch my head, but when I did, a surging pain went through my side. "Ow. God. What's that?"

"Probably your stitches…she thumped you pretty good."

"Who?" I asked. I honestly couldn't remember.

"A girl named Megan, but don't worry, she's in maximum security now and they said she won't return to your floor."

"Oh. What are the stitches for?" I tried to lift up my shirt, but it hurt too much.

"Um…she was stabbing you with scissors when the nurses found you."

"She was? But how…?"

"Apparently she lifted them from a nursing assistant and had them hidden in her room. They think she was going to kill herself, but I guess she decided to try them out on you first."

"Oh."

"Sorry, bad joke."

"Yeah. How long have I been in here?"

"A couple of days. You were unconscious for a while, but you've come in and out of it. You had to have surgery for the stabbing."

"My throat hurts."

"The doctor said it will take a while, but you will get your voice back, so don't try and talk too much."

"How are the kids?"

"They're good. They're at my mother's. I'll bring them to visit tomorrow."

"Um...do I look, OK? I mean, I'm not going to freak them out or anything, will I?"

"It will be fine...they just want to see you."

"Bring me a mirror would you?"

"Nah, not just yet...just rest for now."

"Please, Michael."

"All right, but you're a little swollen, so don't get upset." He went into the bathroom and came back with a small mirror. He set it, face down, on my legs.

"Now, before you look, I want to tell you something."

"Michael..."

"Shut up will you? I have to say something. I was angry at you for a long time. During this last year, I blamed you for all of the trouble and I was embarrassed by you...I know that sounds horrible, but I was."

"Thanks," I said.

"No, I...what I'm trying to say is that I don't blame you entirely now. I sat through those hearings and read the stories in the paper and was so mad I was glad that you were sent here. But I've gone through things. I've looked at all the papers and I know now that I am partially to blame. I let this happen and I let you take it all - the blame, the worry, the anxiety. I know that now."

"Michael, I don't want to talk about this..."

"No, I know. And we don't have to, not right now. But I need you to know that I know, that I understand and that when this is done, we'll be OK. OK?"

"OK." I didn't want to argue. How could I when he was being so loving, so understanding, after all these months? "Can I have the mirror now?"

"Sure."

I looked into the mirror and was almost unrecognizable. My face was puffy and red, my eyes bloodshot and there was a dark ring around my neck with what looked like two distinct thumbprints at my throat.

"Charming," I whispered and handed back the mirror. "Maybe we should wait a couple of days on the kids."

"No...it will be OK. They won't mind. I'll warn them, OK?"

"OK. If you think they can handle it...you'd know better than me these days."

"Carrie...I..."

"No, it's good. I'm fine. Why don't you go get something to eat and I'll see you tomorrow. Tell the kids I love them."

"Alright," he said as he kissed me lightly on the forehead. "I'll see you tomorrow."

I was glad he was gone. It felt terrible to feel that way, but just seeing him and knowing that he would be going back to the kids and I wouldn't was almost too much to bear. It was kind of ironic, in a way. I was sent here because I intended to never see my children again and now all I wanted to do was be with them. But it wasn't as if they were the reason I wanted to kill myself. They were the only reason I almost didn't try.

I loved everything about being a mom. I didn't mind the diapers and the spit-up and the constant feeling of being wet that one gets when she first has a baby. The crying and colic, none of it bothered me. What bothered me was being poor.

Michael had a good job. It was a steady position with an independent, start-up lab and he loved it. But it paid horribly. It was enough to get by on though, barely, so I didn't say anything and constantly called my mother for pasta recipes and hints on how to make kids love oatmeal. When Madeline was about two, I decided to get a job, but Michael wasn't in favor of the idea. He didn't want Maddie to go to daycare thinking that with all of his hours away at least one of us should be with them all of the time. Since his job, even as low-paying as it was, would pay more than I could ever make waiting tables or even working for the local paper, I agreed.

But every time I bought another 90 cent box of pasta at the store or denied the children a day out because of lack of cash, I thought about ways I could make some money. And I'll admit, I was jealous of the Stepford Wives. I was jealous of their new SUVs and their children's brand new clothes without patches over the holes in the knees. The only reason their kids had holes in the knees of their pants was if it was in style to have them there. No one ever said anything, that I heard, derogatory about my impoverished status, but I felt beneath them just the same. I recognized my jealousy for what it was. I knew in my head that "money couldn't buy love" and all of that other crap, but I was tired of paying the Visa bill with the Mastercard and the car payment with American Express. I was tired of disconnection notices from the phone company and the electric company and frankly, I was tired of having to say no to everything from dance lessons to soccer because it all cost money.

So I tried a million "make money from home" schemes. I tried Web sites and assembling products from home. I tried to create a mail-order catalog and to sell and buy real estate. It was crap - all of it.

Maddie, Jack and I were at a birthday party for one of Maddie's playgroup friends on June afternoon and as usual, I was taking pictures. My good old Canon was still in great shape and I took pictures as often as I could. The house was filled with black and whites of the children and Michael even converted a closet in the basement into a darkroom for me. It was an expensive hobby, however, so I spent more time on simple color photos I could have developed at the drug store than on developing them myself. As luck would have it, although I didn't know it then, the hostess's camera had dead batteries and I was asked to the pictures. Terrified that I wouldn't have enough money to develop them, I set about taking all of that standard shots: kids around table, birthday boy opening presents, blowing out candles. But I also had a great time following the children around the yard and catching them at odd moments, like when a butterfly would land on their arm or when they found a bug on their cake.

I dropped the pictures off and during the next week, my phone was ringing off the hook from every mom within the school district who had heard I was an "excellent photographer."

It was sheer luck, but within a month Carrie Connor Photography was open for business. I didn't have a studio, but instead invested in some basic lighting equipment and traveled to the homes of the elite. I called them "environmental portraits." I took posed pictures of families in front of their fireplace or on their front porch. Sometimes we went to the beach and I would pose the families or just the children, dressed in their Sunday best, on the sand dunes.

I was good at it. I was good at getting the kids to smile, even the little ones. More often than not, Jack and Maddie came along. It was hard in the beginning, they always wanted to be in the pictures, but eventually they got the idea.

The best portraits were of just the kids. I would tell a small child to show me things in their yard, a flower, a rock, something like that and then I would ask him a question and when he looked up to answer, I would take the picture. This worked really well with kids who didn't want their picture taken and it was much better than the studios and their puppets. Usually, I could get four or five different shots before the child caught on and ran back to his mother.

So my life was perfect, relatively speaking. I didn't make a lot of money, but I made some and I was loving being involved and having something besides laundry to do everyday. People called us and invited us to things. For the first time in my life I felt like I mattered to people outside my family.

I woke up the next morning, blinked a few times and found myself still on the medical ward. I was genuinely surprised to find myself still there.

"Oh, good," a nurse said. "Your awake. You have a visitor."

Oh please God don't let it be Michael with the children, I thought. I nodded my head and looked out the window.

"Hey sexy," a familiar voice said. I looked up to see Val standing over me, Nurse McLaughlin behind her.

"Debbie here said I could come visit you," she said.

"I'll be right outside you two," Debbie said. "No funny business, OK Val?"

"Yes, ma'am," Val said, trying her best to look sheepish. Val couldn't quite pull off sheepish - she always looks to sinister.

"How is everyone?" I asked.

"The same. Sheila went ballistic last night after her boyfriend came for a visit," she said. "She's in solitary again. And hey, I just got out of there, so I have to be good. Well not completely. Here." She threw me a pack of smokes.

"I don't know if I can do this in here - what if I blow something up," I said.

"You won't," she said and pulled a cigarette for herself out of the pack. Her hands were raw and scratched. I was about to touch one, when she snatched her hand back and sat back in a chair.

"No big deal," she said. "I had a bit of trouble pulling that psycho off you."

"Are you all right?"

"Well, I've been in solitary for the last week, if that's what you mean," she said. "First they thought I was in on it with Meghan and then they kept me in there for going in her room."

"I'm sorry," I said.

"No worries," she said. "I was tired of them anyway. I needed a break." She got up and started poking at things around the room.

"I was in here once," she said. "Right after I had my baby."

I froze and then tried to be cool. This was new information. No one had ever heard Val talk of a baby before.

"Really," I said. "How long were you here?"

"Three or four days. Then right to the ward," she said.

"How old is your baby?" I asked. Val stared at me and then walked to the window.

"Well, I guess she would be about four now," she said.

Four? I thought. Val was just nineteen. She was fifteen when she had a baby? Don't act shocked, I thought. Fifteen year olds have babies all of the time.

"Would be?"

"She's dead," she said.

"I'm sorry," I said.

"Yeah, well, it's weird you know? First I didn't want her, then she was gone, and I did."

"God," I said. She sat back down in the chair.

"I was going to give her up for adoption, but…"

"Go ahead," I said. "I won't tell anyone."

"Christ, it's a pathetic story, really," she said.

"No more pathetic than anyone elses, I'm sure," I said.

"Yeah, well, my mother married this guy," she said, "And like all the guys she went out with, he was an asshole. But I was used to that. I was used to the guys crawling into bed with me, trying to feel me up. Whatever. But this guy had a son. He was like 20 and he would come over and drink, but I thought he was kind of cool.

"So, one night, he and his buddies take me out to a party and whatever, whatever, and it gets late and we're all drunk and they rape me. Out behind some old house, in the woods."

"Jesus," I said.

"So, I got pregnant and I was going to have an abortion," she said. "But I got talking to some lady at the family center and she told me that I could still have it and put it up for adoption. I got to thinking that if I could give this baby a really good happy life, then maybe, I don't know, I would send, like, good karma out into the universe and one day, something good would come my way."

"Wow, that's really amazing of you," I said. I didn't know what to say.

"So, I go home and I tell my mother and her husband and they freak, and I left. I stayed at my boyfriend's house and another girl and I went to school for a while but then it was too weird. It's not like I was ever a cheerleader or anything, but it was weird. I had a job at McDonald's for a while, but it was too hard."

"I'm sure - it's hard to be on your feet all day when you're pregnant," I said.

"Yeah, right. You know. Anyway, I was like, a few days from having the kid and so I went home. I don't know why, I guess I just wanted my mother or something. Hoped she would help and all that. But I should have known better."

"What happened, Val?"

"I had the baby in my mother's bedroom and she helped. It came really fast. I always thought labor was supposed to be long, but this kid came fast. Like it was shot out of a cannon or something."

I smiled. Val smiled back.

"My mother's about to take me to the hospital when the asshole comes in, sees the mess on his new bed and grabs the baby. He calls me trash and a million other names. Said he wasn't going to let another girl into the world with mine and my mother's slut blood running through it. My mother tried to grab the baby away, but he punched her. He said he was just going to drop it off at the hospital, you know, like that Safe Haven thing. My mother said to let him go. That the baby would be better off. And I did."

Tears were running down Val's cheeks, but she never bawled, not like I would have. She took a breath.

"A few days later, I saw on the news that some kid found a baby in a porta potty at the state park," she said. "And I knew. I knew the bastard had just left her there."

"Oh my God," I said.

"So I killed him," she said. "I took one of the kitchen knives and while the bastard was passed out on the couch, I stabbed him."

Val's hands tightened into fists as she said this. She rolled her fists around like she was reliving the moment. Her eyes were focused on a point on the floor, but I knew it was that couch she was focused on.

"I stabbed him over and over, everywhere," she said. "And when it was done, I called the police and told them to come get the bloody asshole off my couch."

My heart was pounding. I pictured my own children and considered what I'd do if someone tried to hurt them.

"I was sentenced to a year here," she said. "Since then, I come and go. I got hooked on drugs for a while, but now I just smoke weed, that kind of thing."

Then, just as quickly as she told her story, she jumped up.

"I gotta go," she said. She opened the door a crack, turned to me and smiled slightly. "Next time, it's your turn."

I smiled back. I wanted to say something profound. Something to ease her pain, but there was nothing. I lifted my IV inflated hand in a wave and she was gone.

Chapter 6

Michael's illness came on suddenly and looking back, it is probably where the whole thing began, although I didn't realize it then. We were lying in bed one night and he woke up writhing in pain. He kept complaining about his neck and his back. I tried massaging it for him and got a heating pad, but nothing worked. I gave him some Tylenol and tried to get him back to sleep.

An hour later, he woke up, still in pain and sweating from fever. I got up and got an icepack from the freezer.

"Get that thing away from me," he said. "I'm freezing. Jesus turn the friggin' heat up."

I ran and got a thermometer from the medicine cabinet.

"Put this under your tongue," I said.

"Jesus, will you lay off," he said and he rolled over.

"Alright, I'm going to go downstairs," I said. "Call me if you need anything."

Gandhi was a Libra

Michael was a terrible sick person. Absolutely miserable. He hated being waited on, but wouldn't do anything for himself either. Whenever he was ill, I would just go sleep on the couch, which is what I did then.

A few hours later, I heard a thump on the floor. I ran upstairs, thinking one of the kids had fallen out of bed. Maddie and Jack were perfectly fine and sound asleep. I went back to our room and found Michael on the floor.

"Jesus," I said and tried to lift him back into bed. He started convulsing. It was the most frightening thing I had ever seen. His big, strong body lifted and thrashed like it was being tossed about by unknown forces. I thought he was possessed.

I ran to phone downstairs in the kitchen, but the cordless wasn't there. I pressed the pager and after tossing every sofa cushion on the floor and every toy in the toybox, found it lodged beneath the bookcase.

Dead. Shit. I ran to the basement, the only place where we have a wall-mounted phone and dialed 911.

I have no idea what I said to them, but they assured me an ambulance was coming. I ran upstairs to check on Michael. He was asleep - or unconscious. I remembered to check his breathing. He was breathing. OK - the kids. Surely they heard me running around. But no, they were both asleep. I checked their breathing too. Then I saw lights flashing outside. I ran to check Michael and then ran downstairs to open the door.

The paramedics took over. They filled our bedroom and I couldn't see anything. Maddie started to cry. I ran to her and picked her up, holding her on my hip as I watched the paramedics take Michael down the stairs on a backboard. He was dead to the world. He didn't move once.

"What's wrong with him," I asked the last guy down the stairs.

"We're not sure," he said. "Are you coming with us?"

"Yes," I said. "No, I can't. I have to find a place for the kids first, then I'll be there."

"Alright," he said. And they were gone. I brought Maddie down to the basement with me so I could use the phone. Jack, sleepy-eyed and unaware of what had happened, followed us down.

"Mama," he said. "What..."

"Hang on," I said. "Let me call Emily."

Emily only lived a few blocks away and within minutes she was at the door. I put a videotape in for my now fully awake children and tried to explain that Daddy was very sick and had to go to the hospital.

"He'll be better, right?" Jack asked. My "yes" seemed to be sufficient and he settled in for this unheard of 4 a.m. showtime.

"Just go," Emily said, when she came through the door. "Call me when you know something."

I walked quickly through the hospital parking lot, the February wind biting through me. I didn't button my overcoat, but hugged it around me, my arms folded in front. I was still in my pajama bottoms, but had thrown on a sweatshirt and put my hair in quick bun. I could still feel the sleep on my face even though I had been up for hours.

The automatic doors hummed alive as I was thrust from the lonely, dark world of night into the bright action of the hospital emergency room. Though small, the Onion Bay Hospital was alive with activity. People in the waiting room, pacing, a man angered by a vending machine, a baby crying, small children running around. I approached the front desk.

"Hi," I said, in my calm and cheerful voice, "Is Michael Connor here?" I knew he was there, of course, but I didn't know what else to say.

"Yes," the nurse said. "Are you his wife?"

"Yes."

"You need to come with me," she said. She pointed to a door that buzzed when I walked to it. She was on the other side when I walked through.

"This way," she said. I followed her through a maze of halls and curtains, some full, others dark and quiet. At the end of the hall, we stopped.

"Put this on," she said, handing me a mask.

"What's this for?" I asked.

"Just put it on, the doctor will explain everything."

"Alright," I said, but I fumbled with the masks ties and it slipped down around my neck. The nurse, obviously frustrated with my ignorance, turned me around and tied it.

"Go in there," she said, pointing to a curtained section of an otherwise empty room.

I walked over and peered my head around the curtain. Michael was lying, still silent, on a bed with tubes running in both of is arms. Completely stripped, he had ice packs all over his body and a tube up his nose.

"Umm, hello?" I said, hoping one of the several nurses and doctors would notice me.

"Are you Mrs. Connor?" a young woman said.

"Yes," I said.

"Will you step outside with me please?"

"OK."

We walked outside of the curtain into the hall.

"Mrs. Connor," she said. "I'm Dr. Vandensteen. I am the attending physician here."

"OK," I said.

"Your husband is very ill. Has he complained of headaches or neck stiffness lately?"

"Yes, the past few days he has had some headaches and earlier this evening his neck and back were hurting," I said.

"I see," she said. "Well, he's resting comfortably now, his fever is down, but I'm afraid he might have contracted a strain of meningitis."

"Isn't that…" I choked on the words, "Isn't that fatal?" I was whispering now.

"Not always," she said, putting a hand on my shoulder. "It's very likely we have caught this early enough and will be able to treat him. We need to run some tests, send his blood to the lab, that kind of thing. Do you have children?"

"Yes…two."

"OK, you and your children will need to come in for a dose of Rifampin," she said. "If it is meningitis, that should keep you from getting it."

"OK," I said. I was starting to feel lightheaded.

"Now, one more thing," she said. "We'll have to know who he's been in contact with, through work and that kind of thing, so that they can be notified and given medication as well."

"Oh my God," I said. "He meets so many people, all of the time. He just held a lecture in Madison for the environmental studies department. Oh my God." I was starting to freak out. All of those people. How were we going to contact all of those people. What if they all had it? Was it my husband's fault?

"Hang on, hang on," Dr. Vandersteen said. "It's quite possible that if your husband was at the university than he wasn't the only one who contracted it. We will contact the public health department there. Calm down. You don't need to do all of this by yourself."

"OK, can I see Michael now?"

"Yes, but not for long, alright?" she said. "He'll have to be moved soon and then after he's settled, you can come back."

She led me back to Michael. The urgency of the doctors and nurses wasn't quite as apparent as it was. Maybe the worst was over. I leaned over Michael's face and kissed him on the cheek. I could feel the tears coming, but I didn't want to cry - not yet. I ran my fingers over his forehead, then down his eyes, like my mother used to do when she was trying to relax me into going to sleep. I carefully avoided the tube in his nose and touched his soft lips with the tip of my finger, tracing each one slowly.

Gandhi was a Libra

Michael and I were always close, but since Maddie had been born, we had treated each other more like the best friends we were than as a couple in love. As in most marriages, I expect, the urgency of sex diminished and we didn't grab each other the way we used to. I had even, on occasion, fantasized about other men or wondered what it would be like not to be married. Not because I didn't love Michael, just because I wondered. But right then, as I looked on the face I had looked at everyday for the last 10 years, I couldn't imagine him not being there. I couldn't imagine a day without him in my life and for the first time in a while the love welled up inside me until I felt like I would burst if I didn't just hold on to him. But I couldn't. And now a nurse was telling me to go so they could move him.

I walked out of the room in a daze, wandering down halls, looking for exit signs until I found myself in the lobby again. I started heading out the doors, when I heard a voice call me.

"Mrs. Connor?"

"Yes," I said.

"You have to fill these out," she said, thrusting a clipboard full of papers in my hand.

"Yeah, OK," I said, but I don't have any of my stuff with me.

"Just do the best you can for now," she said and pointed me toward an empty table with some pens on it.

Filling out the papers, I realized one thing: Michael didn't have insurance. Shit. We had gone on the state's plan for mothers and children when I was pregnant, so the kids were covered because the premiums through his company were huge. Michael really wanted to buy our house as an investment, so we kept the state plan in favor of getting insurance through his company, keeping as much money in his paycheck as we could.

God, could they turn Michael away? No, they couldn't now, he was already here. They had to treat him, right? They took an oath or something. I'd have to figure it out later. A payment plan or something. OK, that sounds good, they must do that. Not everyone has insurance. I dropped the forms off at the desk and told the nurse I'd be back soon.

"You'll have to speak with the business office in the morning," she said as she looked over the forms.

"I will, first thing," I said.

The drive back to the house was short. I opened the window in my car even though it couldn't have been more than 20 degrees. The cold air felt good on the tears falling down my cheeks. I had to keep blinking them away so I could see the road.

When I got back Jack, Maddie and Emily were all asleep in front of the television. The movie they were watching had finished but the TV was still lit up - the only light in the room. I put an afghan over the three of them, touched Maddie's face and walked to the kitchen. I was going to make coffee, but I sank to the floor and cried until my throat was so swollen I could hardly breathe.

Chapter 7:

Michael was in the hospital for a month. I visited him everyday with Emily's help, but things on the homefront were going down hill fast. Because Michael hadn't taken advantage of his insurance opportunities, like disability, I was maintaining the household finances on credit cards and trying to get more business.

I walked into the hospital one morning, several weeks after Michael had been admitted and made my way confidently through the halls. Mr. Vickery from the business office stopped me in the hall before I got to Michael's room.

"Mrs. Connor," he said. "How is your husband?"

"About the same," I said. "Thanks for asking."

"About your account..." he said.

"I know. I'm sorry. I am working on it," I said.

"We need to get it up to date," he said.

"Alright, let me see what I can do," I said. My heart was racing and a pit opened up in my stomach. Go away, go away, go away, I thought. It had only been a little over a month and already they were hounding me about the damn bill. He wasn't even out of the hospital yet. Weren't bills supposed to be for services rendered? Not being rendered...

I tried to put the anxiety of the mounting bills out of my mind as I approached Michael's room.

"Hey Baby," I said. "How's it going today?" I sat in my chair, stroked his forehead and ran my fingers through his hair.

"Planning on waking up anytime soon?" I forced myself to be cheerful. And as if he had done it everyday for the last month, he blinked awake.

"Oh my God," I said. "Hi. Hi. You're awake." He smiled.

"Let me go get a nurse," I said. "Hang on."

I ran out into the hall and called for a nurse. A nurse, Dr. Vandersteen and what appeared to be a team of medical students ran in behind me. They pushed me aside and poked at Michael, asking him question after question.

"What? What?" was all Michael said in reply. I could see his head through the mass of white coats, turning wildly. Suddenly, Dr. Vandersteen told everyone to leave. I stayed and watched as the crowd filed out.

"Michael," she said, looking into his eyes, "Can you hear me?"

"What?" Michael yelled it this time. He was confused and obviously angry.

Dr. Vandersteen took out an instrument and looked into each of Michael's ears.

"Hang on a sec," she said, raising her finger into a number one position for Michael to see.

I took the opportunity to sit by Michael and hold his hand. I looked at him and mouthed "I love you." He settled back in his bed and glared at the wall.

Dr. Vandersteen returned with another doctor, who looked over Michael.

"Carrie," Dr. Vandersteen said. "Meningitis, as we've talked about, can have some serious side effects. One of those is deafness. Obviously, that is what has happened to Michael."

I was stunned.

"Is it...permanent?" I whispered.

"There's no way to tell right now. It's probably temporary, but it could be permanent. We'll have to wait and see."

"So, what does he...what do we do?"

"Well, we'll run some tests and try and figure out to what extent his inner ear is damaged and then we'll take it from there. I'll schedule him for occupational therapy and they will teach him some basic signs to help him get along for now."

"OK," I said.

"Try not to worry," she said. "Like I said, it could be temporary."

Dr. Vandersteen and the other doctor left us alone. I grabbed a pen and paper from the nightstand. Michael reached for it.

"Well, this sucks," he wrote and then he smiled as he passed it to me.

"Yes, but you were very sick," I wrote. "This is nothing compared to the alternative."

"True enough, I suppose," he wrote. "How are the kids? What day is it?"

When I wrote the date he was genuinely surprised. We filled the entire notebook that morning and I promised to bring him more notebooks and a book on sign language. That was just like Michael to want a book right off the bat. Always the academic. But despite his initial anger, he was taking it surprisingly well.

"Only temporary, I'm sure," he wrote before I left to pick up the kids at Emily's.

"Me too," I wrote. It was the last time I saw him that I could still be considered relatively normal.

I noticed a clicking sound in the car as I pulled out of the hospital parking lot, but chose to ignore it. Emily could tell something was wrong when I went to pick up the kids, but I didn't tell her anything except that Michael had woken up. With many smiles and a promise to come by for dinner later in the week, I drove the car the five blocks to our house. Not five feet from the driveway, the car stalled and I coasted it in to the garage.

"Shit!" I said. Jack and Maddie looked at me, startled by my sudden rage. I tried to start the car again, but there was nothing.

"Crap," I said. "Let's just go in the house and have dinner. I'll think about it later."

Jack and Maddie were perfectly happy with this reasoning as they ran to the door. They dropped their stuff in the hall and requested a cartoon.

"You can watch Sesame Street," I said, knowing full well what was next.

"Can't we watch Nick Jr.?" They asked.

"No," I said. "The cable is broken. Just watch PBS and I'll make spaghetti."

"OK," Jack said, "but Mom, aren't I little old for Sesame Street?"

"Jack, you're six," I said laughing at his precociousness. "How can you be too old for anything?"

"But Mom," he said, "they teach letters on Sesame Street and I can already read. I am reading Harry Potter, you know."

"Yes, I know," I said. "Watch it for Maddie, OK?"

I felt guilty. I knew it was only TV and there were plenty of children in the world who didn't have food, but not having enough money to pay the cable bill was really grating on my nerves. Between that and the car, I thought I'd have an aneurysm.

The cable and the car were the least of my problems, however, because when I woke up the next morning, the power was off.

"Fuck!" I yelled, when I discovered that the water didn't work when the electricity was off. Neither did the cordless phone. I set Maddie and Jack up with some cold cereal (use the milk, quick, was all I could think), grabbed an old electric bill and went downstairs to the good old wall phone.

I called the number and tried to negotiate a payment plan. Apparently, it would have worked had I called the day before they shut off the electricity, but after it had been shut off, they needed full payment. It was a $500 bill and I had just maxed out my Mastercard paying the gas and phone bills. My other credit card only had $400 on it and I was using it for food and gas and to pay the other credit card bill.

The money I made from my last portrait job I put toward the mortgage and I had avoided the public service bill because I knew they couldn't cut you off in the winter. But it was the beginning of April now and they could cut me off whenever they wanted.

I called my father. Calling my father was going out on a limb. Our family was close, but when it came to money, it was always every man for himself. My father never loaned money to friends, he said. Even as a child, I never received an allowance and there were very few chores which could net me any cash. He always said that helping around the house was not paying work. It's not that he was particularly strict, he was great fun as a dad, but his attitude about money was very rigid. My parents were also a lot older than a lot of my friend's parents growing up. My mother was 60 when I graduated from high school and my father almost 65.

"Dad," I said. "I'm sorry to bother you at work, but I need some help."
"What's up?"

I told him everything. He already knew about Michael, but I hadn't told him about the lack of insurance - knowing that he'd think we had been very foolish, which, obviously, we had. I told him about the credit cards and the power and when I was done, the other end of the phone was silent.

"Dad? Are you there?"

"Yes, Carrie," he said. "I'm here. But I don't think I can help you right now. I just don't have any extra money. Your mother was just put on another medication and our insurance didn't cover that. I also had to get a new car. Darling, if I could, I would. Let me see what I can do."

But I couldn't. I just couldn't push him.

"OK," I said. "But Dad, don't worry about it, OK? I'll figure something out."

"I'll talk to your mother and call you tonight, OK?"

"OK, thanks Dad, I appreciate it."

"You bet. Hang in there."

I hung up the phone and stared at it. What now?

"Mom?" Jack called down the stairs. "Is it time to go to school yet?"

Shit. The car.

"Um, yeah," I said. "Let's walk today."

It was a long walk, a little over a mile, but I figured Jack could do it and Maddie I could put in a wagon.

I bundled the kids up and headed out the door - back to my cheery self, declaring this an adventure. And so we walked, and in my melancholy, I still found time to help Maddie examine sticks and keep Jack from walking too far ahead or too close to the road. As we approached each street I called out, "Stop at the sidewalk!" And he did. Jack loved to be the leader on our walks. He pretended to be a tour guide and would point out places of interest - like the yard sale where we got his bike or the road to the neighborhood playground.

I tried to enjoy these moments with my children. I was very conscious of the fact that they would grow up all too soon and I would long for these days, but the nagging of the cold, quiet house pounded my brain. Through my smiles, I was trying to figure out how I could cook and live until Michael's next disability check came. He was getting disability, but it was barely enough to cover the mortgage, much less pay for electricity and food too.

OK, OK, I thought. If I use the Mastercard for food and take $200 out on it, plus take $300 from Michael's $700 check for the electric bill, then I should be able to pay that plus almost half of the mortgage. That could work. OK, but what about next month? Well, the electric bill will be lower...and, oh, who cares, I'll figure that out then.

Gandhi was a Libra

We finally made it to the school. Maddie and I walked Jack to his classroom quickly because we were obviously late. I hung up his stuff in his cubby and pushed him in the door, smiling big and apologizing for his tardiness to his teacher.

"We decided to walk!" I called. Mrs. H. - her real name was apparently too complicated for first graders to pronounce - smiled back and waved. I knew there would be no problem. We were some of the good parents. The parents who always volunteered, always returned permission slips and the myriad of other papers on time and who always changed their children's clothes and brushed their teeth before they went to school in the morning.

Many of the children in Mrs. H's class were not so lucky. Several had to have field trip permission slips pinned to their shirts when they left in the evening because their parents - or whoever looked after them - never opened their backpacks, if they had backpacks. Most wore boots and coats five sizes too large for them, or two sizes too small and never had a new pair of socks. It was so sad to see and I tried to read to them and make them feel wanted, but the sad truth was that a lot of these children were already angry. Too angry for six-year-olds and they could take it out on my child. When they did, by hitting or pushing or tearing clothes, I would get angry back and forbid Jack to play with them outside after school.

It was hard to see the life lessons these children had already witnessed, but at the same time, I didn't want my child to witness them too. Although, I must admit, several of these little boys, barely six, with no one home for them after school, would let themselves into our backyard to play on the swings and I let them stay. I didn't always let Jack out with them and when I did, I sat there, watching, but I felt guilty that their own parents had let them down. I also made them take books home and made them promise to read them and give me a report the next day.

Sometimes the books came back, sometimes they didn't. I didn't care.

As Maddie and I walked down the school hallway to begin our long journey home, Phyllis Layton popped up behind us.

"Carrie? Is that you?" she said. Oh Christ, I thought. Phyllis was the preeminent Stepford wife. She was always beautifully manicured and crisply dressed and drove about town doing her doctor husband's errands in her sporty little coupe. She had two perfect children and sent her children to public school instead of private because she believed it supported the community. She was in the cadre of women who made up all of the activities in school and I had taken the pictures at her daughter's birthday party.

"Hi Phyllis," I smiled. "What's up?"

"Well, you wouldn't believe the luck of finding you here this morning," she said. "We are just starting to pop the popcorn for the sale at the end of the day - you know to benefit the music program - and we need one more person to help, and here you are!"

"Here I am," I said. And so Maddie and I followed Phyllis to the cafeteria where the popping was to begin. Really, I didn't mind the diversion - it was much better than facing the idea of cooking all of our meals on the grill for the next few weeks…or longer.

The volunteer moms were all ready popping when we entered. Maddie ran around the room and played with the doll she never left home without as I took place as the taper of bags. Each bag had to be taped closed and placed in a box for each teacher's room. The children pre-ordered their popcorn bags the week before and received them on Friday afternoons.

I looked around the cafeteria and spotted Emily, my one friend in Onion Bay, across the room, struggling with a five gallon bucket full of popcorn. She half waved and smiled and pointed to her youngest son so Maddie could have a playmate.

I actually began to enjoy myself. The women were happy and talked about their children and their husbands. I was shocked to discover that Phyllis was a Star Trek fan and could actually contribute some to that conversation.

Another mom, Joan, asked us if we had seen a new show on the Discovery channel. I tried to spin my current television-less state by claiming that we rarely watched TV. It worked.

"Oh, I don't watch much either," Joan said, almost defensively. "We keep it to educational shows mostly - except when Tim needs to watch the Packers."

All the mothers laughed at this. The Packers were ingrained in the fabric of all of Wisconsin. For however many Sundays in the fall and winter, the whole state ceased movement to watch the Packers play.

"We are going up north," Phyllis said, "just as soon as the weather gets warmer. The cottage must be just a wreck - we haven't been there since last fall."

"Oh ours too," Joan said. "It's supposed to warm up next weekend - I should really get out there and clean."

"I don't know how you girls can go up north," another mom, Amanda, said. "I simply hate going to the country. My idea of roughing it is when the curtains in the hotel don't match."

"Hah! I know just what you mean," Phyllis said. "No, no, it's not rough at all - it was, don't get me wrong. But we renovated it and now there's a pool for the kids and the lake view is just beautiful."

After every comment, Emily and I would look up from our jobs of taping and sorting and roll our eyes. Emily was one of the few mothers I knew who had a regular job. She managed a restaurant and so was available in the mornings for volunteering and field trip chaperoning.

"And sleeping," she said.

"It sounds wonderful," Amanda said. "How about you, um...Carrie? Do you like camping and all that?"

"Actually, I do like camping quite a bit," I said. "That's what you're left with when your husband's an environmental scientist, I guess. But I'd love a vacation at a five-star resort someday!"

They all laughed and despite my horror at their attitudes about, well almost everything, I kind of like that they were talking to me and making me feel welcome. I hadn't found many friends since moving to Onion Bay and I was rather enjoying the sensation.

Of course, the long walk home brought me back to reality - my reality - and as Maddie and I grilled our hotdogs on the back porch, I was raging with jealousy. It came out of nowhere. Why did they get to have cottages and brand new cars? Why did they live in huge historic homes while I struggled just to get this tiny bungalow paid for? I wanted that life.

Chapter 8:

I cried myself to sleep that night. It was the first of many nights and I started taking Tylenol PM to get myself to sleep. When I ran out of that I took the last of the Benydryl and then the Nyquil. Each night of the month Michael was in the hospital was a torment of crying and plan hatching.

And then Michael came home. Finally, I thought, things will get back to normal. His disability checks began to arrive, but they were paltry compared to his already small salary. A mere $150 a week. Enough to turn the lights on, but little else.

Phyllis was an unknowing savior and unwitting accomplice early one morning after I dropped Jack off at school. I was still walking - the car immobile in the garage.

"Hey Carrie," she called as I walked down the hallway.

Oh Good Lord, I thought, another popcorn popping event? Between looking after Michael and the children and trying to rob Peter to pay Paul, I was out of energy for even the smallest volunteer efforts.

"Hey," she said, catching up with me. "I have something here for you." She handed me an envelope full of cash.

"What's this?" I asked.

"Don't you remember? It's the money for the pictures of the fifth and sixth grade baseball teams. You're supposed to take them next Wednesday."

"Oh yes, of course," I said. "Excellent. What time is that again?"

"Gosh you must be busy - it's 4 p.m. at the field."

"How many teams are there?"

"In the league - must be at least 10, with 15 or so kids per team."

"Right. Great. Thanks," I said and started walking out. In my hands was a fortune. An absolute fortune. But unfortunately I would get to keep only $300 of it. The rest would go towards film and prints. But I had credit at the store...

No, stop, I thought, walking faster down the sidewalk, the cash safely in my purse. Just put it in the bank and do your job. You can't play that game. I walked directly to the bank and deposited the money into my business account, but I did advance myself the $300 - something I rarely did - in order to have some food money and maybe work towards paying to have the car fixed.

I walked home and found Michael asleep on the couch, Maddie quietly stacking blocks on his chest.

"Hey guys," I said. "How's it going?"

"Daddy's sweeping," Maddie said.

"Yes, I know honey, let's let him sleep." Michael was awake when I left, but I made a note not to leave Maddie with him for so long next time. He was apt to just drift off at any moment these days and I didn't want her to get hurt.

I started cleaning the kitchen and mentally planning for the photo shoot the next week. I was also scheduled for a daycare center later on in the week and a dance school over the weekend. All in all, the photo business was doing well and if Michael were able to work, I'd be able to save money. But it's always something isn't it? He was bound to feel better soon. The doctor said it could be six months or more before he felt himself again. I knew I was lucky he was alive and to have him home, but I was also impatient for him to get better…I didn't like that I was impatient, but I couldn't deny it either.

I went to bed that night, as I did every night, alone. Michael's body was still racked with pain and it was easier for him to stay on the couch. It was probably better that he didn't see me tossing and turning. My heart palpitating over the phone calls that would surely come the next day.

Everyday they began, bright and early at 8 a.m. Calls from credit card companies, the insurance, phone, utility companies, informing me of my lateness, of my impending cancelled or "referred to collections" accounts. I had taken to clicking the phone in the on position and shoving it in the cushions of a chair so Michael couldn't hear the beep of a phone off the hook.

When he asked me how things were, I lied. I told them everything was tight, but fine. He had so much to worry about just getting better, I didn't want him to feel forced to go back to work.

A call from the bank took me by surprise one morning.

"Mrs. Connor?"

"Yes," I said, thinking damn, I forgot to click the phone off.

"We've had trouble reaching you," the woman said.

"Really?" I acted surprised.

"Yes, you are now two months behind in your mortgage payments."

"Is it two months? I'm sorry, I've been out of town…" I thought sounding like a lady of leisure - unconcerned by those mundane little bills might save me.

"Yes, well, we need your payments by this Friday or we'll have to take further action."

"Further action?"

"Yes, if your mortgage goes in arrears for much longer, our foreclosure department will be in touch."

"Oh, well. Don't worry," I said. "I'll come in by Friday."

"Thank you Mrs. Connor."

"Oh no, thank you," I said.

Fuck….Fuck. It's all I could think. Had it really been that long since I paid the house payment? God, I guess it had. I got out the checkbook for the house and then my business checkbook. Maddie and Jack were playing in their playroom making a ton of noise, but I was ignoring it. Michael asked me to tell them to quiet down.

"Why don't you tell them?" I said. "I'm tired of telling them. It's cold out, they can't go outside, what do you expect them to do?"

"Fuck off," Michael said. "I'm tired."

"You're always tired," I muttered under my breath. I didn't mean it, but I did.

Jack came thundering down the stairs.

"Mom, can I…?" Jack said.

"What?!" I screamed back. "What do you want now?"

"Nothing…" he said and started to slowly walk back up.

"Jesus Carrie, what the hell…" Michael said. "What do you need Jack?"

"Nothing, never mind…" He went upstairs. I felt bad, but not bad enough to go after him - not yet.

"Good Lord Carrie, what is the matter with you?"

"Nothing, OK, nothing," I said. "Just lay off me for a minute."

"Fine."

"Good," I said.

I took the checkbooks into the kitchen and sat down. Family balance: $350. Photo balance $3500 (all designated for film and prints). Mortgage due: $3200, including the upcoming month.

I could do it, I thought. I could pay it right now and not have any problem with the bank. We'll be in good and have a place to live. Maybe then I could get a loan for the pictures, but they won't give me a loan unless I pay the bill. I had to think about it. It sounded too easy…and it was kind of stealing, wasn't it? No, I would replace it. It was just borrowing.

Briefly relieved, I went upstairs with a handful of cookies and some juice and made friends with Jack again.

"I'm sorry, buddy, " I said. "I was having a bad day."

"You sure were," he said.

"Will you forgive me?"

"Uh huh, but don't do it again," he smiled, knowing he was using a grown-up term.

"I promise," I said, crossing my heart.

I tried to make up with Michael too, but it wasn't easy. I rubbed his back and brought him dinner, but he was still sore. It was partly my fault. I told him it was PMS that was bugging me, not the bank. I don't know that it would have changed anything either way. Besides, Michael can hold a grudge longer than anyone I ever known. I can't hold a grudge to save my life. I blow up and then I want to be friends again. I hate having someone angry with me. And I hate being angry - it takes too much energy.

Michael once held a grudge against me for a week all because I called him a "Son of a Bitch." To me, it was just a friendly swear word, to him, I had personally affronted his mother who had been dead for several years at that point. I felt terrible about it, but couldn't see why he had taken it so personally. It seemed silly, but I never called him that again. And he forgave me eventually. He was close to his mother and she died very young, so I guess I understood.

Michael was also a terrible sick person. He was the most loving husband in the world, but when it came to anything - a cold, the flu - anything. He was miserable. Just a laying on the couch, telling us all to move out from in front of the TV and not make so much noise tyrant. It was the complete opposite of how he was normally. Any day of the week, Michael would come home from work, give the kids a bath or make dinner and always helped with laundry or whatever. I always thought that I could never make it as a single parent because Michael was such a great husband. I couldn't imagine how single moms did it on their own. Every night, back when he was working, I desperately looked forward to Michael walking through the door at 5:30 and giving me a much need respite from Maddie and Jack.

I slept on my own for the first time in months. I had a plan of attack. I would get us out of this mess. I would transfer the money from my business account into the family account and call the bank in the morning. They could take their payments and we would be in the clear. After I took the pictures for the different teams, I would put the prints on my credit account at the photo lab and it would be fine. I could use Michael's disability for food and then next week I'd apply for a loan. No problem.

Chapter 9:

What is it they say about the best laid plans?

"Hmmm?" Dr. Leslie was watering her plants and pretending not to pay attention to the silence in the room. I had been released from the medical ward a few days earlier, nearly three weeks after the "incident" as Nurse McLaughlin likes to call it, and was having my first therapy session since my return.

"I didn't say anything," I said.

"I thought you said something about plans?" She asked.

"Did I say that out loud?" I lit up a cigarette. Since the incident I had practically become a chain smoker, smoking late into the night, lighting one cigarette off the other, hiding the butts in a soda can (diet and uncaffeinated of course) in my closet.

I couldn't sleep. The three weeks in the medical ward they took me off most of the meds they gave me to cope with being in this place in order to take medication to keep me from dying. I wasn't sure which was worse. As the memories of what I had done flooded back, after somehow being suppressed beneath my haze of meds, I couldn't bear to breathe again.

It's not that I didn't know or couldn't remember why I was in there. The drugs just made it so I didn't really care. Once I had been off them - with all that time in the hospital bed to think - I couldn't stand myself again.

"I feel like I'm back at square one," I said. "Like I haven't accomplished anything."

"Maybe you haven't," Dr. Leslie said.

"What do you mean? What kind of thing is that to say? You're supposed to tell me I'm getting better."

"I am?"

"Aren't you?"

"I don't think I'm supposed to tell you're better, Carrie, I think I am actually supposed to help you get better. Until you talk about why you're here…"

"I know, I know."

"So, if you know, what are you asking me dumb questions for?"

"I thought there were no dumb questions."

"Whoever said that didn't work here."

"Something you want to talk about?"

"Hmmm…" she said, almost smiling. "You need to decide something Carrie."

"What's that?"

"You need to decide if you are going to be able to face up to what you did and go back out there and live your life again or if you are going to hide in here and continue to deny you did anything wrong. You need to either own your behavior or not. If you just want to chalk it up to bi-polar disorder and sleep it away, you can do that too."

I lit another cigarette…off the end of my first and stubbed the other one out on Dr. Leslie's floor. She pretended not to notice. Maybe she didn't.

"Go on back to your room and we'll see how you're feeling tomorrow."

I wanted a Valium and I wanted to go to bed. Every time the image of my past popped into my head, I winced. I couldn't squeeze it out. The embarrassment, the pain I caused, I just wanted it to go away.

I missed the kids. And Michael. But I felt safe in there.

I sat on my bed. Janet wasn't there. Must be in the showers, I thought. It was rare for her to be gone in the middle of the day. People kept peeking in on me, "just to be sure I was OK." At least four people, Val included, had come in to inform me that Meghan had been taken away - where no one knew.

I reached over to my bedside table for the shoebox I kept there. It had pictures of the kids, drawings and cards they made me, a picture of Michael walking out of the bay looking very muscular and very tan. At the bottom was a small pile of newspaper clippings. I hadn't looked at them in the six months I had been in the hospital. I felt compelled to look at them now. To somehow face what I had become. And there I was, on the front page of the newspaper, crying and looking absolutely hideous, sitting at a table in the courtroom, being told to spend the next year of my life in a mental institution - or else spend two years in jail.

It was amazing how fast it all came apart.

Let's just say my plan wasn't at fool proof as I had initially thought. I made the transfer between accounts and then dutifully paid the mortgage. Then I went a little farther than I should have: I bought groceries and got the car fixed. I also took out a small ad in the newspaper advertising my photography skills, but I chalked that up as a business related expense (as I did the car) so I didn't feel too guilty about that.

Then I just went about my days as if nothing was out of the ordinary. Michael got a little stronger each day and I got up and took Jack to school, then took Maddie to whatever photo shoot I had planned for the day. I took any job: a wedding, a child's portrait, a headshot for the newspaper. And then I went home and did what became my own version of accounting.

The money came in and I paid our household bills with it and charged the photo supplies and prints. I was nervous each time I did it, sitting at the kitchen table, trying to figure out who to pay and how much to get me by until the next month, but I was in control. For almost six months, I was completely in control. Looking back, I think I was addicted to the adrenaline rush - it was my own form of gambling, but I didn't know that then.

I acted completely normal on the outside. I went to school events, continued to volunteer in Jack's class, went to Tupperware and Pampered Chef parties. Emily and I hung out and drank wine on Friday nights while the kids played in the backyard. I was doing it, I was going to get us out this mess. I started sleeping on my own again.

Normal started to seem a lot less normal when the bank didn't approve my request for a personal loan.

"We're sorry Ms. Connor," the woman at the bank said over the phone, "but you seem to be too overextended right now for us to approve your loan."

"But isn't that the point of a consolidation loan?" I asked, trying not to sound nervous and the borderline hysterical that I was quickly becoming. "To help me not be overextended anymore?"

"Well, yes, but coupled with your history of late payments, it's just not a good idea. After you have established a year or so of consistent, timely payments, we will be able to reconsider your application."

"Um, OK," I said. I wanted to point out the hilarity in this logic, but it didn't seem to be the right time.

"Is there anything else I can help you with today?" she asked. Why do they always ask this? Isn't it obvious she didn't help me out with the first thing I asked for?

"Um, no, thanks," I said. My heart started pounding. If I didn't get the loan, I couldn't pay off my credit at the photo lab and they had all as much said that I wouldn't be able to get more credit for the prints I had pending. I had three jobs in there now, waiting to be paid for and delivered. And I had already spent the money paid to me. Shit.

Michael started teaching at Onion Bay Community College and the pay was decent, enough to keep up with our bills, but not enough to pay the nearly $5,000 I owed at the lab.

I went to bed with my head reeling. How was I going to fix this? I had taken so much money - stolen all of this money, in essence - and now I couldn't make good on the photos I had taken. I still had myself convinced that I had just borrowed it, but deep down I knew that wasn't the case. My heart pounded and I woke up continually throughout the night in cold sweats. I'll just make small payments, I thought. The lab will have to understand, I'll have to make them understand. What if they don't understand? What if they don't understand? What if everyone finds out what I've done?

Then it came to me. All at once, like a shot, and I was immediately calmed. I'll just kill myself then. It wouldn't be so hard, a handful of pills, a deep sleep. It would be so easy to just let it all go.

What about Jack and Maddie? What would happen to them? Don't think about that now. Michael would take care of them and he has his parents and mine. They'll be fine. They'll be better off without you, Carrie. I cried, silently, and fell asleep watching Michael's chest rise and fall.

Each day went by in a haze and I continued to act perfectly normal on the outside and fought with myself on the inside. I saw Phyllis and Joan almost everyday and my heart pounded while they asked me about ordinary things like my plans for summer vacation or what station I wanted at the end of the year school fair.

"Oh, wherever you put me is fine," I said.

"Great," Phyllis said, "just come a couple of hours early to help set up and we'll see what we have."

"OK, great," I said. I went home everyday and filled out new applications for credit cards, not realizing until it was too late that each application was another nail in my already coffin-like credit report.

Everyday I prayed the mail would bring me a new credit card that would get me out of the hole I kept digging and everyday another bill arrived for one I had already maxed out and couldn't afford to pay.

Although my façade worked well in public, I couldn't mask my nerves out home. Every ring of the phone had me jumping out of my skin and every time Jack or Maddie innocently walked up to me on the couch, I snapped.

"What?" I yelled.

"Can we watch Blue's Clues?"

"Yes, sure, fine, whatever," I said.

"Jesus, Carrie, are you all right?" Michael asked me repeatedly.

"What? Oh, yes, I'm fine. Sorry, must be PMS."

"If it's PMS, you've had it for a month now," he said.

"Have I?" I was trying to sweeten my tone. "Sorry."

Summer vacation came, and I thought I'd be safe for a while. No encounters with any of the Stepford Moms, but then the phone began to ring.

I avoided it easily enough during the day, carefully screening my messages and returning only the calls that offered work, but at night it was a different story. Michael would answer the phone, I knew, not knowing about maxed out credit cards or people waiting for pictures. So I did the only thing I could do, I took the phone off the hook downstairs in the basement, so he couldn't hear it. If he had to make a call, which he rarely did at night, I could easily blame it on Maddie playing with it in the basement while I did laundry.

The mail was just as scary. I couldn't let him see the bills or bank statements either. I sorted and hid the mail that would be shocking to him before he got home and on the weekends I practically pounced on the mailman. If there was anything bad in the Saturday mail, I left it in the box until he wasn't around, when I could open it and deal with it myself.

Gandhi was a Libra

There was no angle I hadn't considered when trying to cover up the damage I had done, both to my customers and our own finances. We were out of the woods now as far as utilities were concerned, but I had shot our credit rating during his time out of work. He probably would have understood maxing out the cards and getting new ones. He was out of commission for a long time, but I had so tied up the cards with the transfers I had been making that I couldn't see how I could explain one without explaining the other. The only solution was to keep them both a secret until I could figure a way out of this mess.

Still, at night, I comforted my nauseous stomach and pounding heart with thoughts of suicide. I conditioned myself into falling asleep to the feeling of throwing myself off the top of a building or laying coatless out in the woods in a not uncommon 30 below Wisconsin winter night.

Chapter 10:

I remember July 23 vividly, but after that it's all a blur. Leslie said we would work on that, but I knew what was there. I just didn't want to look at it. I woke up late. A habit I had gotten into since school let out. I would worry all night, take some Tylenol PM I hid behind the bed to go to sleep and then wake up groggy and drugged at 10 or 11 a.m. Jack and Maddie were wonderful. They got up at eight and went downstairs. Jack made them cereal and they played and watched PBS until I dragged my ass out of bed. Michael left for work around seven, so he never saw my ineptness.

Even as I laid there in bed, listening to them play, I couldn't get up. I dozed in and out and thought about what I had done - and what I had to do. I cried a lot. Then finally, after I had worn myself out crying and dozing, I got up and went downstairs. The kids were always fine, happy to see me, but their happy faces compounded my guilt. I was guilty. Guilty of sleeping too much, crying too much, hiding too much. I sat there on the couch next to them, a cup of coffee cradled in my hand, and would reaffirm each morning how they would be better off without me.

Gandhi was a Libra

July 23 was no different. But then it was. The phone rang incessantly. And this time it wasn't a creditor or the electric company. It was Phyllis, then Joan, then a woman from the daycare center. Phyllis had contacted them, all three messages said, and they were curious what was "up" with the photos I owed them. It had been two months. They wanted to meet with me.

Shit. I unplugged the phone.

I sat on a chair in the living room and shook with fear. I was on the verge of crying but hadn't started yet. Shit. They're going to figure it out. If they haven't already. I'm fucked. I started to look frantically at the bills and my "system." I just needed one more big job, I thought, then I could pay for the pictures still waiting at the lab. But I was out of time, I knew. I was going to have to explain it all. There was only one thing left to do and that was follow up with plan B.

I couldn't. I couldn't do it. I was chicken, pure and simple. I could not face them all and tell them what I had done.

"Jack," I said, "honey, go get your backpack and bring it here. We're going to Grandma's."

"Yea!" Jack and Maddie said, happy as can be. They dutifully brought their books and movies to me and I packed them up. I packed us each a small bag and then I asked them to play for a bit while I did something.

I wrote two letters. One I wrote to Michael. I explained everything, but told him I'd be back in a couple of days. "I just needed time to sort it out," I wrote. The other I wrote to Phyllis, explaining what I had done. I apologized profusely in my shaky hand and then sealed and mailed it before I could change my mind.

And then I drove. I drove slowly, crying most of the way, with Jack and Maddie laughing and yelling in the back. I stopped at a lake with a small public beach and let them wade in to their knees and play in the sand while I contemplated my fate. I just needed a few more days with them, I thought. Then I could do it. It felt good to be at this lake. No one knowing where I was. Or who I was. I was the woman who had stolen nearly $15,000 from her customers.

After a couple of hours at the beach, I found some peace with my plan. I took a deep breath and realized I was doing the right thing. Suicide was my only option. I calmly called the kids back to the car and dried them off. I turned back on the road toward my parents' home and arrived an hour later.

They were surprised by our sudden arrival, but hugged us and brought us all in for dinner.

"What brings you down here?" My dad asked.

"Oh, I don't know," I said. "Just felt like getting out of Onion Bay."

"Excellent, excellent," he said. "Well, we are glad to have you. Is Michael coming down?"

"No, not this time," I said. "He has a lot of work to do and we were getting a little antsy."

"Sure," he said. "How's the photography business?"

"Good," I lied. "Not too much to do when school's out. A couple of weddings here and there - nothing huge."

"Well, as long as you put away some of your money for the dry times," he said.

"Sure Dad," I said. "I try. It's hard with these guys, of course."

"I know, I know," he said. "But it's important. Every little bit helps."

This was a common conversation with my father. The money talk. He was forever telling me the best places to save all that spare cash I should have. Of course, I never had any, but this didn't seem to dawn on him. Usually, I got into a huge argument with him about it, but not this night. On this night, I calmly listened and found his conversation rather endearing, knowing I'd never hear it again. I watched closely as he gave the kids extra large slices of cake or slipped them a dollar bill. He promised to take them fishing the next morning.

Gandhi was a Libra

My mother hovered over all of us with extra helpings of pasta and salad and asked me about the Jack's school. She knew I didn't have a lot of money, but she let my father go on. She asked how Michael was feeling since his illness.

I played the good daughter, for once, and answered all of their questions. I had no energy to argue over anything and let little comments like, "Shouldn't you be home taking care of Michael?" slide. I didn't used to. I used to get snotty, then angry, when they made their comments. But on this night none of it mattered. After dinner, when Maddie curled up on the couch with Gramma to read, I did the dishes in silence, confident that they could be happy here. Michael could come see them all the time if he couldn't take care of them himself. Between him and my parents, and his, they would be fine. Happier. Better off.

I noticed Michael didn't call me that night. I wasn't surprised exactly, but I was thrown off. I couldn't remember ever not saying good night to him in the seven years we had been married. It was unsettling, but I fell asleep that night easily, curled up on the floor between Jack and Maddie. And for the first time in months, I didn't wake up at 2:01 or 4:35. And the next morning, I didn't sleep in. Proof positive, I thought, that I had made the right decision.

What I didn't know then, and didn't learn until a couple of years later, was that Michael was going through a separate kind of hell. While I was off getting a good night's sleep, he had been kept up late into the night by my angry customers. A few called, but Phyllis and Joan came over and together, they apparently reconstructed what I had done. Michael freely gave them as many of my records as he could find. The bulk of which I had actually stashed in my backpack before I left. He also found the bank statements and credit card statements and was shocked by what he learned. How, he wondered, had I kept it all a secret for so long? And why? It had seemed so obvious to me at the time. How could he not understand it?

Michael went to bed that night with promises from Phyllis and Joan that they would get the police involved if restitution wasn't made soon.

The morning of July 24 was hot and muggy. My father took the children, as promised, down to the pond by his house to do some fishing. And I, oblivious to what Michael was going through, told my mother I had some shopping to do. She agreed to watch the kids for the day. I promised to be back in the afternoon, but I knew I wouldn't be. I hugged the kids tightly before they left, reminding each that I loved them more than anything. I hugged my mother too and then got in my car for the long, three-hour journey back to Onion Bay.

I cried most of the way. I prayed to God to look after my little ones. I begged Him to forgive me for what I had done and what I was going to do. I stopped only once during the drive, at a drug store, to pick up my weapon of choice.

I drove into town paranoid that someone would see me. Phyllis wouldn't have gotten her letter yet, I reasoned, so no one but Michael would know what I had done. Of course, that was before I found out about the previous night. I opened the door to my house. My beautiful, little house that I had fought so hard to keep - even if I had fought in all the wrong ways. I walked around, taking a final look at everything and clutching my bottle of Vodka and box of sleeping pills.

I went into Maddie and Jack's room. I laid down on each of their beds. I wanted to cry, but the tears wouldn't come. I was all cried out. I pictured their faces as babies and tried to imagine what they would look like at their high school graduations and their weddings. I imagined the grandchildren I would never see and a lump formed in my throat. I went to my room and got a pad of paper and pen from the nightstand. I wrote them each letters, telling them how much I loved them and how what I did wasn't their fault. I wished them the best lives and told them I would look over them. I also told them to listen to their father and to enjoy their lives. Above all, I wrote, I want you to be happy and remember I will always love you.

I wrote Michael a short letter, apologizing and telling him how much I loved him. And I did. As much as I knew I needed to get out of this life I had created, I also knew that I loved Michael more than anything. What a wonderful man, he didn't deserve a fuck-up like me.

I folded each letter and placed them on my bed. Then I walked calmly to the guest bedroom with my vodka and pills and sat down on the floor. I opened the vodka and took a swig. Ick. I had never tried straight vodka before. Should have bought some orange juice, I thought, but then, that would have diluted it. It occurred to me how odd it was to be having this conversation with myself right before killing myself. I popped all of the pills out of their foil packages. There were fifty in all. Ten handfuls of five.

I took five of the pills and swallowed them all with a sip of vodka. I never had any trouble swallowing pills, I thought as they went down, even those horse pills they call prenatal vitamins. Five more pills and another swig. Then five more.

That's all I remember about that.

I do remember waking up in the hospital and feeling like shit. I was weak and I felt like I had recently been used as a punching bag. Michael was there and my mother.

"What am I doing here?" I asked, whispered is more accurate because my throat was raw as well.

"Shhh…" Michael said, "Don't try to talk. They just took the tube out."

"What tube?" I asked.

"Shhh…"

My mother smiled at me and then left the room, returning with a nurse, who in turn left and returned with a doctor. The doctor approached the bed.

"You had us all worried," he said. "How are you feeling?"

"Like I went three rounds with Mike Tyson," I said.

He smiled. "You still have your ears intact though, so you're doing OK." He looked at the machines and I.V.s around my bed, made some notes on the chart and then left. I looked around the room. There was a large window to my right, looking out on the nurses' station.

"Nice view," I said.

"They have to keep an eye on you," Michael said. "Make sure you don't do anything…" He was going to say crazy, but he stopped himself. It was then I remembered everything that had led me here. Michael sat on the bed and held my hand.

"I didn't mean to come back," I said.

"I know you didn't."

"Where are the kids?"

"At my parents. They're fine. Missing you."

"What's to miss?"

"Plenty," Michael said, looking right in my eyes. "And you'll see them soon."

"I don't know," I said. "They don't deserve a mother like me." I turned my head away and stared at the wall opposite from the nurses' station. It was too much. It was supposed to have ended and now it was all back again - and everybody knew. It would have been different if everybody had found out and I was gone, but this was intolerable. I didn't want to be alive with the knowledge of what I had done.

"Christ," I said to the wall.

"What?" Michael said.

"I couldn't even kill myself right." He squeezed my hand and brushed the hair out of my face.

I didn't know it then, but I was already in the medical ward at the Adams County Mental Institution on the outskirts of Onion Bay.

Chapter 11:

Michael visited me everyday, sometimes with the children. On this day, he left the children at home and brought instead a detective from the Onion Bay Police Department. His name was Clive Krueger, he said, and he was just there to talk.

He had in his hands copies of the letters I had sent to Phyllis, Joan and the daycare center, confessing my crime.

"Now, they are some pretty angry women," Clive said, "but I want you to know that we are not yet certain a crime has been committed. However, if there is anything you can tell us…"

"Shouldn't she have a lawyer?" Michael asked.

"Now, now," Clive said. "I just want this to be as informal as possible. I'm just saying that if there is anything beyond what's in the letters we should know, then you can tell us."

"I don't think so," I said. "Not really. But everything's a little fuzzy right now."

"All right," Clive said. "I'm sure. I just want you to know that what we will probably do is pass this along to the district attorney and he will decide what to do with it. As for the police department, we will most likely recommend that you're charged with felony theft."

I looked away. This was too much reality. Michael talked to Clive some more and escorted him out.

"We'll get a lawyer," Michael said. "Don't worry - it's not like you have a record or anything."

"Hmmm…" I said. "I need to sleep."

"You just woke up," he said.

"So, I'm still tired."

"You're always tired."

"Leave me alone."

"We need to talk about this," he said.

"Talk about what? The fact that I need a lawyer? How are we going to afford a lawyer? The only reason I'm in this is because we couldn't afford anything and now we need a lawyer too?"

"Yes," Michael remained calm. He was always calm.

"Fuck that," I said. "It was my money. They gave it to me. Fuck that."

"But it…"

"Fuck it," I said. "Leave me alone." And to emphasize my point I ripped out whatever tubes were in my arms, causing the whole room to go up in a blur of squeaks, alarms, bells and whistles and subsequently, a battalion of nurses got up from the station and ran into my room. Michael slipped out with them. I flopped back on the bed, smiled sweetly at the nurses and apologized. I looked at my arms. I hadn't noticed, but they were black, blue and bloody. Blood was seeping through my sheets and onto my gown. All the nurses put on their rubber gloves, just in case and then they redressed me and the bed without me ever getting out of it.

I continued to make nice, smart-ass comments, but they only looked at me and smiled. When the doctor appeared minutes later with a fresh syringe to calm me down, I knew what those nurses were smiling about.

I soothed myself back to sleep that night in my same old way, thinking about jumping off buildings and taking pills. I laughed at myself over the taking pills idea. I'll have to take more, faster next time. But how was I going to get a hold of them? Whatever was in the syringe took over too quickly and before I could formulate a plan, I was asleep.

In the morning, I awoke to the sound of Michael talking to yet another strange male voice. They were sitting at the table in my room, drinking coffee.

"Hello?" I said.

"Hey there," Michael said. "This is John Hansen. He's the assistant district attorney."

"Oh," I said. "Hi."

"Hello Carrie," he said. "I'm glad to see you're doing a little better."

"Hmmm…" was all I could manage. "Could I have some water?" Michael came over to my side table and poured me a cup.

"Can you sit up a bit?" he asked.

"Yeah, OK." I pushed the button on the side of the bed until I was mechanically brought up to a more congenial height.

"All right, Carrie," Mr. Hansen said. "Now, I don't want you to be upset by all of this and I want you to know that we are going to do everything we can to make this painless."

I snorted in contempt and immediately regretted it. Michael looked at me disapprovingly, but Mr. Hansen smiled.

"No, really," he said. "The facts in your case are really pretty solid, but we also know that you don't have any kind of record and that you are obviously dealing with some pretty serious…issues.

"The various groups that are pressing charges are pretty angry, but I don't think they really want to see you do any jail time, and quite frankly I can't see that that would do you any good. So here is what I am recommending."

This is all going too fast, I thought. Jail time and prosecutors, holy shit, I had no idea it would come to all this. I couldn't even believe it was me they were talking about. Me, good little Carrie O'Connor who never walked against a red light and always crossed in the crosswalk.

"Yes?" I asked.

"I am going to give you this advice, if you can get at least $12,000 of the amount you owe back to those you took it from before the end of August and we'll reduce the charge to a Class A Misdemeanor and we won't recommend jail time as your punishment. Probably you'll receive a couple of years of probation." He might as well have told me to pay back a million dollars. Where was I going to get $12,000 in one month?

"But, I can't guarantee that, ultimately it's up to the judge. Even a misdemeanor can bring as many as three to five years in jail."

"Oh," I said. Michael was just nodding his head.

"It all depends on the judge," Mr. Hansen said.

"I see," I said. "OK."

"OK," he said. "So, you work on getting the money together - borrow from family and friends if you have to and then at the end of August we will reevaluate your case. For now, you just concentrate on getting better."

"Umm...OK," I said. My mind was a blur. All this information made me want to do was kill myself again. Fuck this, I thought. Fuck this.

I sank back into my bed and Michael saw Mr. Hansen out.

When he came back, he sat next to me on the bed.

"That doesn't sound so bad," Michael said, holding my hand.

"Are you kidding? Where are we going to get $12,000 in a month? Fuck. If I could have done this right, we wouldn't be here right now."

"Stop," Michael said. "Will you please stop? I am sick of hearing you talk about killing yourself. It's very tiresome."

"Oh," I said, "I'm sorry if I'm annoying you."

"Look," he said, trying to calm down, "I'll figure it out. I'll talk to work and our parents. Somehow, we'll get it."

"Yeah, whatever," I said.

"You need to relax. It's all of this anxiety that got us here. You need to learn to deal with it."

"Oh, it's my anxiety that got us here? It wouldn't have been you being out of work forever? No, of course not," I said. "It's all my doing. The fact that you were on the couch for six months had nothing to do with it."

"I know, I know, but you could have told me..."

"And what, demanded you get out of bed and go to work. You were sick for Christsake."

"Yes, but stealing Carrie..."

"Oh, shut up," I said. "I don't' want to hear about it. I know what I did. I thought it would work, OK? If I had had more time it would have."

"You don't still honestly believe that?"

"No, I honestly believe I would be better off dead."

Michael left. The commitment papers came that afternoon. I didn't even have to sign them, Michael and a psychiatrist who had been observing me all ready had. All I had to do was move when I was well...physically well.

" A month?" I screamed at him when he came to visit the next day. "Michael, you can't seriously want me to stay in this hell hole for a month?"

"It's not that long," he said. "I talked with a lawyer and she said that if you spend the time here the judge will look more favorably on you, first of all. Second, you need the help, Care, you need to get past this suicide bit."

"It's not a bit," I whispered.

"I'm sorry," he said, getting in bed next to me. "No, it's not a bit. But you know what I mean."

"Why are you still here?"

"What?" he asked, turning my face to look at his.

"Why are you still here? Why haven't you left me yet?"

"I don't know."

"Hmmm…" I said, falling asleep again. I couldn't answer that any better than he could.

My lawyer came to visit the next day. Suddenly my room had become Grand Central Station. Michael was there, but she asked him to leave for a bit. He looked at me and smiled.

"I'll be back soon," he said.

The lawyer walked over to me put out her hand.

"Hi, I'm Jane Lelyveld," she said, shaking my hand.

"Hey," I said.

"Your husband's very nice," she said. "He really cares about you."

"Does he?"

"Yes, he's working very hard to get the restitution together. That should put us a long way in the judge's eyes."

"That's good," I said, thinking, It's about time he worked to get some cash together. It wasn't a very kind thought, I know, but I was glad the burden finally fell to him.

"OK, let's see," she said, flipping through some papers in a folder on her lap. "Assuming Michael gets the money together, we'll face the judge for an initial appearance the first week in September."

"Do I have to go to the courthouse?"

"No, for that, you'll appear on a monitor from here in the hospital," she said. "You'll plead not guilty, at first, that will give us time to work on a deal with the D.A."

"But I am guilty," I said.

"Well, now, let's not say that just yet," she said. "We'll plead not guilty which will give us time to work out a deal and also give you time to be evaluated by the psychiatrists here. Then they can make a recommendation that should keep you out of jail."

"Oh, that's good, I guess," I said.

"Look, I know this is all very overwhelming," she said. "But everyone is working hard to see that you get through this, OK? You have a lot of sympathy on your side, no matter how angry the victims in the case are."

"How angry are they?"

"Well, most of them aren't so bad. The parents of the kids you took pictures of have all just expressed an interest in getting their pictures, not seeing you go to jail, which is good. But one woman, Phyllis Maynard, is leading a very hard press to have you punished. She wrote a letter to the D.A. saying that you two were best friends and she felt very betrayed."

"Really?" I said flatly. "Phyllis is my best friend now?"

"She said she was, is that not true?"

"If she was my best friend, then I was never let in on it."

"I see. Well, that's really of little consequence. But it is the main reason this is going so far. Normally, in a case like this, we can get this settled without going to trial."

"I don't want a trial," I said. "If I plead not guilty, don't I have to go to trial?"

"Not necessarily, in your next appearance, you can change your plea to 'no contest,' which will avoid a trial and get you sentenced right away."

"Oh." This sounded like a bigger clusterfuck than I could handle.

"Don't worry," she said, patting my arm, "we'll get you through this."

"Sure," I said.

"I've got to go. I'll be in touch over the next few weeks."

"OK," I said. "Thanks - I guess."

"Sure," she said. "We'll work it out."

I fell asleep, again. I don't remember waking up until what was apparently a few days later when Nurse McKinley came to take me to my new home: the second floor.

"What is going on?" I yelled as Nurse McKinley started packing my things.

"Time to go to your own room," she said. "I hear you'll be staying with us for a while."

She said this in the tone of front desk clerk.

"I want to stay here," I said.

"No, no, now," she said. "This room is for someone else now. You're doing better and we need to move you to where you'll be staying."

"Why can't I stay here?"

"Because this is for sick people, and you, lucky girl, are not sick anymore."

"No, I feel terrible, I want to stay."

"Don't worry, there are plenty of beds and people to look after you on the second floor. Besides, you'll meet some new people and make some friends."

"I don't want any friends."

"Well, hopefully that will change." She came over to me and started unhooking all of my tubes. Then she tried to pull me up out of bed. I pulled away and started screaming, "Let me go!" I didn't think I was making that much of a scene, but I guess I was because two large orderlies came in and held me by the arms. They tried to get me into a wheelchair, but when they let go, I ran out of the room. I didn't even know where I was going - or why - but I had to get out of there. Thinking about it now, it reminds me of the time I took Maddie to get her shots. She saw that needle and just flipped out. There was no way she was staying and she ran like the wind toward the front door of the clinic. She was just leaving. A little three-year-old, no idea where she was going, but she knew she had to get out of that place. That's exactly how I felt just then.

Someone caught me. I fell. They picked me up and carried me, still kicking and screaming, to the second floor where they tossed me - quite literally - into an isolation room. A bed, a blanket and a nurse sitting in a chair at the door. There was also a security officer posted at my door in case I decided to run again. I didn't. I stood there, looking at my cinder block room with the mattress on the floor. I don't know how long I stood there. It felt like hours. Finally, I curled up on the mattress and cried. I cried and cried until I fell asleep.

I slept for days, waking only briefly to drink some water or get a shot of something that put me out again. I don't remember using the bathroom, although I suppose I must have. Maybe I didn't. I also remember trays with food being brought in but I don't remember actually eating. Sometimes I wasn't asleep, but I pretended I was. I looked at the wall. I counted the cinder blocks. Even at night, when all the other lights on the floor were turned down, mine remained on. A single fluorescent strip far out of my reach.

Sometimes I just lay there, staring at whoever it was watching me. Now there's an interesting job, I thought. Watch me in my room. I wonder how much they get paid to do that. It's probably a government job with full benefits. I want to die.

Sometimes I could see the other girls roaming around in the hallway. They would try and peek in until Nurse McKinley shooed them away. Eventually, I roamed the halls a bit with my escort. I went to the bathroom and was disgusted by the image reflected back at me.

After my first romp around the second floor, Dr. Leslie came for her first visit. I stayed curled on my mattress the whole time. She gathered her wrinkly rayon animal print skirt around her and sat cross-legged next to me.

"I'm Dr. Leslie Sherman," she said. "You can call me Leslie."

"Hi," I whispered.

"I think you're ready to move to your own room," she said. "You have some appointments to prepare for and it would be better if you started taking care of yourself."

"Uh huh."

"So, Nurse McLaughlin here is going to help you get settled into a regular room and then we'll have a talk, OK?"

"OK," I said. I didn't really care. But I was eager to get up off the floor.

"Alrighty then," Dr. Leslie said. "I will see you this afternoon."

"Alrighty," I said.

Nurse McLaughlin, Debbie, came in and helped me up off the mattress. She gave me a full tour of the facilities. I saw the girls in the TV room, the smoke room, the shower room and the bathroom. All unfamiliar. All soon to become my second home. She took me into my room. A lot of my stuff was already there. A few pictures of Michael, Jack and Maddie were taped onto my closet door, a comforter from home was on my bed, and some familiar knick-knacks off the desk in the living room were on my new dresser.

Nurse McLaughlin introduced me to Janet, my new roommate, who was in bed and would remain there for most of the time I knew her. I sat on the bed, trying it out as if I was in a mattress store and then just sat there, staring at my new surroundings.

"Let's go get you a shower," Nurse McLaughlin said. I dutifully followed her down the hall, looking at my feet the whole way. I could feel the stares of the other girls as I walked. We stopped at the linen closet first, which Nurse McLaughlin unlocked before slipping in for a towel, a washcloth and new scrubs for me.

In the shower room, Nurse McLaughlin kindly instructed me to get undressed and place my clothes in a laundry bag with my name on it.

"Are you staying?" I asked.

"Yes, I have to these first few times," she said. I got undressed with a boldness I had not possessed since birthing Maddie - when you are naked and simply don't care who sees you because it hurts too much.

I tentatively step into the pounding hot water, carefully not to slip on the tiled floor, which does not distinguished between where the bathroom floor ends and the shower space begins. Nurse McLaughlin sits on a stool a few feet away with a bar of soap, a washcloth and a bottle of shampoo in her lap. After I rinse what must be two weeks worth of sweat, tears, grime and smell off of me, she hands me the washcloth and the soap.

I scrub every inch and am surprised by my own body. It's thinner than I remember, but the skin on my stomach still sags from my pregnancies - even though they were more than a couple of years ago. That skin just won't go back. I've done sit-ups and crunches and all sorts of dumb, Ladies' Home Journal/Redbook/Stop the Insanity exercises designed to make my post-natal body look like it was 16 again, but it doesn't. I push the washcloth across my stomach and can feel the muscle there, but the skin doesn't agree. It just sags, stretchmarks looking sad to exist without a purpose beyond pissing me off whenever I look at them. My stretchmarks are a silvery gray now and even though they aren't painful, I still hate to touch them. I especially hate it when Michael touches them. They just make me feel...oogy.

Even now I push the washcloth past them quickly determined not to linger there too long. After I soap up and rinse off at least three times, Nurse McLaughlin hands me the shampoo. I lather up my hair and am shocked to realize, again, that there is far less of it than I remember. I must have looked puzzled by it because Nurse McLaughlin smiles at me.

"You were trying to tear it out," she said.

"What?" I asked.

"Your hair, when you first got here, you were trying to tear it out, so we cut it short so you couldn't get as good a grip on it."

"Really…" I said. I didn't remember any of this. All I remembered was being sleepy. What on earth happened to me in the last few weeks? I finally got out, got dressed in new scrubs and let Nurse McLaughlin lead me back to my room. I laid on the bed and stared at the ceiling. I didn't know who I was anymore.

Chapter 12:

I hadn't been laying on my bed for very long, when the door flew open and a girl dressed in a sweatshirt, baggy scrub pants and bare feet came bounding through. She sat at the foot of my bed.

"I'm Valerie," she said. "What're you in for?" She offered me a cigarette from a pack she kept in her sweatshirt pocket.

I sat up slowly and for some reason, took one. She lit it for me from her cigarette.

"Only the nurses get lighters," she said, "and they only light you up outside or in the smoke room. So you have to smuggle a lit one in. I can do it in my mouth." And she proudly demonstrated how she flipped the cigarette back over and into her mouth.

"Tastes like shit though," she said.

"I can imagine," I said.

"So, what are you in for?" she asked again.

"I'm not sure…" I said.

"Ahh, one of those. We get a lot of that here."

"Oh yeah?"

"Sure, mostly, though, they know, but they pretend not to know, so they can get off faster. It's easier to get out if you pretend you don't remember killing someone than if you remember and just went to the loony bin."

"Oh," I said.

"Come on," she said, bouncing up off my bed. "I'll show you around."

"OK," I said even though Nurse McLaughlin had shown me everything already. What I didn't get on Nurse McLaughlin's tour was Valerie's running commentary - a definite necessity for a newbie.

"Cute kids," she said, looking at the picture of Jack and Maddie on my dresser. "Yours?"

"Um…yeah," I said.

"Alright," she said, opening the door to my room. "Let's go."

She led me down the hall.

"This is the most important room," she said, opening a heavy door with a thick window. The window was criss-crossed with some type of wire. "Security measure. Don't want the crazies breaking the glass." We walked in. There was a card table and several lawn chairs. No other decoration or furniture. A heavy-set girl sat on the windowsill and smoked.

"This is the smoke room," she said. "Hey Rhonda. How's it going? This is…um…what's your name?" Rhonda and Valerie looked at me.

"Carrie," I said and I realized I still had my burning cigarette in my hand, so I took a last drag off of it and crushed it into the overflowing plastic ashtray on the card table.

"Valerie," Rhonda said. "Why were you hanging out with Sheila last night at the movie? I thought you said you'd sit with me." Rhonda looked as though she was going to cry.

"No," Valerie replied, "I didn't. I told you I'd sit with you at dinner - which I did - and that I would sit near Sheila at the movie. Now don't go getting depressed on me. Sit with Carrie and me at lunch, OK?"

Rhonda wiped her eyes, sniffed loudly, like Jack does when he's been crying, and smiled.

"OK," she said. "I'll see you at lunch."

"OK, then," Valerie said. Turning to me, she said. "Let's get out of here."

I nodded and dutifully followed as Valerie then showed me the nurses' station.

"This is where our captors reside," she said, smiling at the women behind the desk. They smiled back. They were not surprised by what I learned was Valerie's normal barrage of insults toward anyone in authority. "If you're good, they might let you have an extra cookie." Everyone smiled indulgently at Valerie, everyone that is, except Nurse McKinley, who glared at her.

"Go back to the main room, please, Ms. Greenburg," Nurse McKinley said.

"Woof," Valerie said and then panted like a dog.

"Why don't you show Carrie the schedule board?"

"Yes Nurse McKinley."

Valerie tugged on my shirt and walked me over to a large dry erase board where all of our names were posted. Next to each name was a variety of initials. Next to mine was "ROF" which Valerie said stood for "Really Off Fucking Rocker" but actually stood for, "Remains on Floor." Most of the names had ROF next to their name, except for Valerie and another girl who had, "AF" next to theirs. "AF" stood for "All Floors," meaning that Valerie could roam the halls unsupervised, but could no leave the building. This was how Valerie kept fully supplied in cigarettes and a wide variety of other sundries. She had no money in her canteen account, so her own version of the black market was the only way she could get by.

We sat down on the couch in the main room and watched Regis and Kelly banter about the morning's news. Valerie played verbal handball with anyone who came near us. I zoned out in front of the television, still in a stupor.

I went along like this for several days - on Valerie's coattails, learning the ways of the floor. I didn't speak very much, but silently observed the women around me. I watched as they fawned over one another and then fought with each other only minutes later. It was a world I hadn't known existed and, despite the circumstances that brought me there, I was a fascinated observer. I did not realize, yet, that I belonged there.

After my transition week, Dr. Leslie and Jane the Lawyer, came for me. Jane the Lawyer suddenly didn't look like the sophisticated attorney I had placed my confidence in while on the medical ward. She looked more like a scared high school student pretending to be the lawyer in a mock trial, who just found out that her client is really a crazy lady from the psycho ward.

"Hi Carrie," Dr. Leslie said. "You need to get dressed, you have to make your initial appearance today."

"My what?" I said, sitting on my bed as Dr. Leslie busied herself gathering the skirt and blouse I was to wear. They were the only normal clothes I had.

"Your initial appearance," Jane the Lawyer said. "We go to a little room down in the basement and we sit in front of a computer and a camera. The courtroom downtown will be on the computer screen - divided in fours - an image of the judge, the clerk, the prosecutors and, well, us.

"It's a simple process, we sit, you answer a couple of questions that we'll go over in a minute, and then you enter a not guilty plea. We sign the bond paper and you're done, for today. Then we'll schedule another appearance - the pre-trial conference - but you don't have to worry about that yet."

"OK," I said, putting on my clothes. Dr. Leslie sat next to me on the bed, tried to help me button my shirt, smiled and nodded.

"You'll be back in a flash," Dr. Leslie said. "Don't let today get you down, we'll talk after, OK?"

"OK," I said. I ran a brush through my hair, it didn't take long to style it, considering there wasn't much of it left.

Jane and Dr. Leslie escorted me down to the basement. I hadn't been down there before. It was a maze of corridors, most of them filled with various arts and crafts projects - most of them in green and gold to appeal to the fans of the Green Bay Packers who occupy every square inch of the state of Wisconsin. Some of the rooms had classes going on.

"This is where the nursing home residents spend their class time," Dr. Leslie said as we walked along. "See, there are lots of different projects they can pursue and then we hold a craft fair in the summer so they can sell what they've made."

"Great," I said, walking by a room where an older gentleman was deftly spinning a pot on a potter's wheel. He looked so peaceful sitting there, his leg rhythmically kicking the wheel around. He would wet his hand and appear to hardly touch the clay at all but it would move, the clay would, and bend to his whim - almost as if he was willing it to and not using his hands at all.

We found our way to the little room at the far end of the basement. An armed officer stationed by the door reminded me of my true purpose - my true identity - to own up to my actions, to be formally branded a criminal.

The officer opened the door for me and Jane the Lawyer. Dr. Leslie hugged me and said to go to her office when I was done. I nodded and walked into the room. The computer monitor was on, but the spaces for the judge and other lawyer were empty. We sat down and waited. Jane explained to me that the prosecutor would talk for a bit, explain the case to the judge. The judge would ask me to state my full name, if I understood the charges against me, and then how I pled. I was to plead not guilty.

After a few minutes, the prosecutor appeared on the screen. He fussed with his papers and his microphone and then sat down, drinking coffee and bantering with the clerk. There were other noises in the courtroom, but I couldn't tell what they were. Much later, I would learn that they were the voices of the women I had offended, watching to make sure I got what I deserved.

The judge walked in and everyone stood. We stood too, even though we weren't there. Jane said we didn't have to, but it was a good habit to get into, and it showed respect for the judge, which never hurts.

The prosecutor was John Hansen, the man who visited me in my hospital room. With the same deliberate demeanor he used to reassure me that he wasn't out for blood, he described my behavior to the judge. The judge then did just as Jane said, he talked into the camera so that he was looking directly at me. Even though I only had to tell him my name and "not guilty," I couldn't help the tears from forming in my eyes.

In a nice, polite yet shaky voice, I squeaked out not guilty and then was excused to go and see my psychiatrist.

Chapter 13:

After several weeks, I am allowed to see the children. It will be the first time they have seen me since I left them that day at my parents' house. Nervous, I paced my room like a caged animal smoking cigarette after cigarette, lighting one off the other like I've been taught by my fellow inmates and tossing the burning butt into a caffeine free Diet Coke can.

We meet in a room on the first floor designated for the purpose. The kids were playing with some old broken toys on the floor when I walked in. Michael stood and met me at the door, hugging me. The kids looked up and ran to me, hugging me and jumping up and down. I sat on the threadbare couch and let them climb all over me and tell me their stories. Jack found out who his new teacher would be. Maddie had a new kitten from Grandma. They gave me pictures they had drawn and begged for me to come home. I was so happy with them on my lap. I was so happy to look over at Michael and watch him watching us.

Where had this feeling been all of these months? Where had the joy in just being with my family gone over the last year? Suddenly, I wasn't feeling shame at what I had done, but shame at what I had done to these two beautiful children. The tears streamed down my face while I smiled and listened and hugged and kissed them. There were going to be tough times ahead, I knew, but I didn't care anymore. Suddenly everything came clear, I needed to get my head back in the game and take care of these guys. What made me laugh - to myself, of course - was I thought that's what I had been doing. All those months of worrying and scrambling were done in the name of me saving the family, but I wondered now if that wasn't just a too lofty excuse for what my mania had become.

I was sorry when the children left that day, but I was more convinced than ever that I was, if not right for what I had done, than at least worth saving. Whatever they threw at me now, I knew I could take it, because the most precious thing in the world was already gone, at least from my day to day life. I resented being in this place and I hated those Stepford Wives for being so adamantly against me, but I'd do it. I'd pay for what I had done and then I'd get on with my life. In this, I was resolute.

Michael kissed me before he left, a long romantic kiss - a kiss I hadn't wanted in a very long time. I pulled back from him, reluctantly and looked at his face. This face that I had loved for so long and then, not loved, covering it in the blame from the last year.

"Why do you love me?" I asked.

"I have no idea," he said. Then he smiled, squeezed my arm and left. I wouldn't see him for another week.

Things became routine in the weeks before my court appearance. I ate with the girls, went to group sessions and had my one-on-one sessions with Dr. Leslie. I spent a lot of time in front of the T.V. and smoking. How did they expect me to get over depression in a place that was so depressing? I alternated between deep self-pity and my resolve to survive this fiasco on an almost hourly basis.

As the days dragged on, I became one with the gray, cinder block décor. I spoke little in group and could not answer Dr. Leslie's probing questions. I dreaded each minute, but when I lay down in bed each night, I dreaded leaving. I was trapped. I did not belong here, among the crazies, but I did not belong out there anymore either...where everyone in town knew who I was and where I was.

Michael tried to keep them from me, but I saw the newspapers. They filtered onto the floor through the nurses desk and the janitors. I saw the small briefs describing me. The photographer who had "taken" her customers. Not all of the newspapers mentioned my name, but the local papers did and that was enough to make me want to die all over again sometimes.

The day of my court appearance, the day I would plead "no contest" to avoid a trial, came quickly. I took my meds for breakfast and was prepped by Dr. Leslie. She gave me tips for dealing with the stress - like taking deep breaths and the visualization techniques we had been working on. Essentially, when I want to think of ways to kill myself, I should go to my happy place. I usually picture the kids playing on the beach or Michael and I in a romantic inn somewhere, but invariably the image is destroyed when Phyllis or one of the other ladies I "tool" as the newspaper so eloquently put it, walks up to our table.

Michael couldn't go to my appearance and I was glad. He had to preside over a public hearing on fishing rights up in the northern part of the state and his mother was looking after the kids. He told me to relax and that nothing would happen that I didn't already know about. He really was being wonderful about everything. It made blaming him seem a lot more unfair, but at the same time, I still held resentment. He got to look like the hero who still loved his demented wife and I got to be, well, the demented wife. I knew his parents and his friends had talked with him about divorcing me. I could tell by the way he talked around the issue of my being in the newspapers. Sometimes it really hurt, mostly I didn't care. It was a strange feeling to not care so much about so many things. I was so used to caring about everything. What people thought, how things got done, other people and their problems, the children. Now I just cared about the children.

I waited for Jane the Lawyer in front of the hospital with a rugged C.N.A. named Bruce. He was tall and had forearms the size of my thighs, but he was gentle as he led me down the stairs and out to a bench to wait. We didn't talk. We just sat and listened to the voices banter back and forth on his radio. When someone swore or said something personal we smiled at each other. When Jane pulled up, he opened the door of her car for me, as if he were my personal assistant instead of the security to protect the rest of the world from me should I have chosen to run away. He didn't come with us, though. Jane told the hospital administration that she trusted me and that if I came to the courthouse "unattended" it would look better for me. Besides, I heard her say the day before, there were plenty of armed guards at the courthouse.

I had never been in the courthouse before. I had been in a building next to it once, a small office where I paid for a bad check I wrote, but never had I walked up the marble stairs and into the big glass doors trimmed with copper. Inside, you were either a suit or not. I was a not. There wasn't much in between. There wasn't a lot of reason to hang out at the courthouse, so you were there for one of two reasons, either you were part of the solution, or part of the problem.

Jane led me to a bench outside of the courtroom door. We sat and she went over what I would say. She told me that the judge would give me an opportunity, after the victim's statement was read, to answer and explain.

"Just be natural," she said. "As long as you are remorseful, you can't really say anything wrong."

"OK," I said, trying to think of something that sounded eloquent and moving. Something Gregory Peckish that would give me the advantage and let the judge see that I was perfectly fine and could go home with a warning "never to do it again."

That didn't happen. What happened was that after the preliminary name recital and my plea of no contest, Phyllis got up and forcefully read a statement that she said represented the people I had hurt.

"We don't think she should go to jail," she read. "But she needs to know that what she did was wrong and if jail is the only option than so be it. She was my best friend and I feel deeply betrayed by what she has done..."

It went on like that for over five minutes. The judge finally stopped her and asked her to turn the statement into the bailiff. Then he asked me if I had anything I wanted to say to the court.

"Um..." I said, and then, without warning I began to bawl.

"I'm just so sorry," I wailed. "I never meant to hurt anyone, I was trying to get my family through a tough time and I thought I could fix it all - I never meant to steal, I only needed to borrow what I took."

Then out of nowhere I started to rationalize a bit through my tears...

"I mean, if I really wanted to steal it, wouldn't I have taken it and runaway to the Caribbean or something. I mean, it's not like I spent the money on shoes, I was trying to feed my family."

I sniveled and wiped my eyes with my hands until Jane gave me a tissue and patted me on the back. I wanted to go on. I wanted to say, "and who does Phyllis Baumgartner think she is anyway saying that she's my best friend. She never once had me over or did anything but give me orders for the school fundraisers," but I didn't. I stopped and just as I was blowing my nose, a photographer from the newspaper snapped my picture. I looked up, startled, and noticed the TV cameras in a window behind the courtroom. Great, I was going to be on TV, too. Probably the lead story, considering nothing interesting ever happened in Onion Bay. If Michael hadn't filed divorce papers by now, he certainly would after tonight's "Coverage You Can Count On."

The judge took a deep breath and shuffled some papers in front of him. Jane was about to say something, but he put his hand up and stopped her. He had kind eyes and grandfatherly glasses. I hoped he said something nice.

"Now, let me just say that what you have done Mrs. O'Connor, is a terrible thing. You have violated the trust that exists not only between a proprietor and her customers but between a woman and her friends."

If I didn't know better, I would swear that I could hear some "Amen's" in the back from the victim's section.

"However," he continued, "I have here the reports from Dr. Leslie Sherman, who confirmed your diagnosis of bipolar disorder. I can only believe that this disease is what has led you to become so ignorant of the laws and morals that govern every other citizen of this country. So, I am suspending the jail term I would normally give of 18 months for a crime of this severity in lieu of the 12 months of continually supervised care that Dr. Sherman recommends for your treatment. When you have completed the 12 months at the Adams County Mental Health Facility, you will remain on probation for two years. If you complete these measures to the satisfaction of the court, meaning you also continue to seek counseling when you are released and remain on any medication you have been prescribed, then you will be free to go and your record expunged of this Class A Misdemeanor conviction. Do you understand?"

"Yes," I said.

"Court is adjourned," he said, and with the bang of the gavel I was free to go back to my new life. For a year. I knew that's what Jane and the prosecutors were pulling for, but it didn't seem so possible until just then. Until then, I had held out some kind of obscure hope that the judge would set them all straight and tell them to let me go. Until that moment, I had been just a temporary visitor on the second floor, now I might as well have been a lifer.

Chapter 14:

Not even during my first few months at the institution did I realize that I was insane. My time there I viewed as my sentence, never as a necessity. I struggled simply to endure, smoking cigarette after cigarette, with no intention of facing a mania I did not believe I had.

I attended group sessions, talked with Dr. Leslie twice a week, wrote letters home to the children, had my visits and never saw it. What I didn't know was how skewed my version of events was. The mania that led me to the financial disaster was only part of it and I had no idea how bad it really was until Dr. Leslie had Michael bring a box into her office one day.

Laid out in front of me on the floor was what I had really done and I was shocked that I had not remembered more. They were doing this, she said, to "shock" me back to reality. To let me in on what was really going on in my head. Until this point, our visits had been cordial. She talked to me about what being a manic depressive meant and I talked about how misunderstood I was and why I didn't really need to there.

"Carrie," Dr. Leslie began, "These are some of the papers Michael has found while you've been here."

"OK," I said picking one or two up at a time and then flipping them back on the floor. Michael was sitting in a chair at the side of the room. I sat on the floor with Dr. Leslie. Michael looked tired, more exhausted even than when he came out of the hospital.

"As you can see, there are quite a few bounced check notices," she said.

"Yes, well..." I started trying to explain, "We were having financial trouble and I was trying to..."

"We know what you were trying to do, Carrie and we both understand. We are not here to judge what happened. Let's take a look at some of the places you purchased things, OK?"

"Yeah," I said.

"There seem to be an inordinate amount of checks written to a local book store."

"Uh huh."

"Do you remember what you bought?"

"Books?"

"Yes, Carrie, but do you remember what kind of books?"

"Not really, probably something for the kids..."

"Well, I thought so too, but Michael found these," she said presenting a sales receipt. "There are a lot of books here."

I looked at the receipt. I remembered this trip. I had seen a guy an infomercial late one night and the guy was talking about making extra money through real estate speculation. I decided that I could get us out of our financial hell by doing this. I went to the bookstore with the intention of buying the guy's book, but ended up looking at the business section and finding all sorts of books on making extra money. While Maddie played with the Brio trains in the nearby children's department, I piled book upon book about restoring credit, 101 ways to make money from home, mail order success secrets and who knows how many more. Actually, there were 14 books on the list. Almost $200 in books that I didn't need or have the money for.

"Why, do you think, didn't it occur to you to try and find these books at the library?" Dr. Leslie asked.

"I tried, I think, but they didn't have them in," I said.

"And you couldn't wait for them to come back?"

"No," I said. "I needed them right then."

"Why?"

"I don't know."

"This didn't seem a little paradoxical to you at the time? That you were spending a lot of money on books that were supposed to help you save or make more?"

"No, not at the time."

"OK," she said. "Does it now?" I didn't want to give in. I didn't want to say it did, even though it did.

"Yeah, a little, I guess."

Michael looked as though he were going to say something, but he stopped. No one said anything. I just stared at the pile.

"All right then," she said, "that's solved for now. What about Christmas?"

"What about Christmas?"

"You applied for quite a few credit cards at Christmas," she said.

"Yes, doesn't everyone?"

"Sometimes. I only ask because you were having such financial difficulty at the time."

"Yes, but I wanted the kids to have a good Christmas."

"Sure, I understand that."

"I mean, how would it be for them if they woke up on Christmas morning and Santa didn't leave them anything?"

"Well, I'm sure that would be a little sad, but what I am more concerned with is just how much they did get a t Christmas."

"OK..."

"For example, you bought a new video game system and a variety of electronics at a department store, plus at least $500 worth of clothes and toys."

"Yeah."

"Well, I also see a receipt for a new stereo system."

"That was for Michael."

"All in all, it looks like you spent over $1,000 on Christmas presents."

"That sounds about right."

"Does it?"

"Well, yeah."

But I knew it wasn't. I knew this was an absurd amount. But I didn't think so at the time. I just wanted to give my family everything they wanted. I wanted Maddie and Jack to have the happiest faces ever. I wanted them to remember me well because I was still convinced I was going to have to die. And I loved buying them things. What I didn't really know and what Michael had apparently told Dr. Leslie was that during my buying sprees I was "unbearable" to live with.

They went on to tell me of how I would stay up until all hours baking or cleaning and then would wake up early with huge plans for the day: volunteering at the school, lining up new photography sessions, going to photography sessions, running errands, shopping, cooking, cleaning. I thought I was being a good mother - they told me I was being "manic."

"How can getting a lot done be manic?" I asked.

"Let me ask you Carrie," Dr. Leslie said, "do people ever ask you to slow down or stop talking so fast?"

"I guess...sometimes," I said, remembering that people have always told me I talk too fast. Even in high school I would constantly be reminded by my teachers to slow down when I was giving an oral report or answering a question. But wasn't that just talking too fast? I mean, I have a lot going on in my mind.

I have always had a lot going on in my mind and sometimes I have to sit down because of it. If I can just stop thinking, I say to myself, I could relax. I always just thought this was the sign of an intelligent person, not that I thought I was a genius or anything, but don't intelligent people have lots of thoughts? I think all of the time. I also dream all of the time and am unable to stop it. I hadn't realized that since I had been admitted, I hadn't dreamt very much and I didn't feel as tired when I woke up. Some days, back at home, I could swear I hadn't slept at all and I remembered vivid, strange dreams. Not particularly weird dreams, odd things, like most dreams are, but just normal everyday things that could easily be attributed to something that had occurred the previous day. But I couldn't stop them. Was this why? For the first time I was realizing that there might really be something wrong with me and it frightened me.

"Carrie?" Dr. Leslie said.

"Yes?"

"Michael is going to leave now, do you want to say goodbye?"

I felt like a small child being told to wave "bye-bye" to Aunt Francine.

"Sure." I stubbed out my cigarette in an ashtray Dr. Leslie had started keeping in her office and got up off the floor. Michael hugged me and whispered "I'm sorry. I love you," in my ear.

"It's fine," I said, smiling, trying to brush off the afternoon's events. "I just thought I was energetic."

"You are," he said, squeezing my upper arms gently. "You are."

Michael left with a promise to return that weekend with the children. I sat back down, on the couch this time and began to light up another cigarette.

"Michael is a very loving husband," Dr. Leslie said.

"Yes, I don't deserve him," I said.

"Now, why would you say that?"

"Oh, isn't it obvious?"

"I think we need to continue for a bit before I let you go for the day," she said.

"Alright."

"You've received a lot of information today. How do you feel about it?"

"What do you mean how do I feel about it? I feel like shit, that's how. I mean, here I thought I was being a good mom and doing good stuff, cleaning and baking, and it turns out that all this energy is because I'm a goddamned lunatic."

"Carrie, it's OK to be angry," she said.

"Good, because I am."

"Alright, why don't we take a break anyway? I'll schedule you in for a special session tomorrow afternoon and in the meantime I want you to attend group in the morning and maybe talk about this anger with some of the other ladies."

"Yeah, fine," I said. I went to the door, consciously stepping on the pile of my financial life. Fuck it. Fuck it all. I was angry, Dr. Leslie said, but was I angry - or manic? I was on the drugs they put me on, so I couldn't be manic right? But how could I ever tell again? How could I ever tell when anger was anger or mania? How was I expected to know the difference? It was all such bullshit. A made-up complex, that's what my father would say. Depression, mania, it was all in your head, he would say, get over it.

But it could explain some things maybe. It could explain the time I was pregnant with Jack and I attacked Michael. We had been arguing over something - who knows what - and he had said something mean, called me a bitch or a fat cow or something and I went ballistic. I pounded on him with my fists, pushed him into the kitchen counter and then grabbed a cereal bowl and smashed it at his feet, shattering the bowl into a thousand pieces. The rage within me was so strong. I could feel it boiling through me and all I wanted at that moment was to hurt him. Not kill him, but definitely hurt him. And as quickly as it came on it was gone. I was suddenly relaxed and calm after the episode.

Together we chalked it up to pregnancy hormones and laughed about it afterwards, but it wasn't the first or last time I would experience such rage. The episodes were few and far between, but frequent enough to now put me on alert. Maybe I was manic. I began to remember more and more instances when I had "raged." A time when my high school boyfriend and I had began to fight in the backseat of a friend's car and me demanding to be let out, on the interstate no less, or else I would jump. I had the car door open when the driver finally pulled over and let me out.

I found a ride with a nice guy in a pick-up truck and after tentatively opening the passenger door and saying, "You're not gonna kill me are you?" accepted the ride to the next town. After wandering around for a bit, contemplating my options, the first one being to call my mother and get a ride (after explaining why I was 20 miles away and not in school), I spotted their car at Kentucky Fried Chicken. My rage swelled again as I stormed to the restaurant, and found the threesome enjoying a nice lunch, probably discussing what a lunatic I was (apparently, I was). I charged over to their table and grabbed my boyfriend by his jacket and pulled him to the ground. I started pounding on him and kicking him, throwing a ring he had given me across the room. The manager of the restaurant came over, pulled me off him and threw us all out. Somehow, once the rage had again left me, we made up enough for me to get a ride home with them. I remember being strangely turned on by the experience and it wasn't long until we were making out his house.

There I was, four months into my extended stay and I was just being to learn how crazy I really was. How had I gone 32 years and never seen it?

Ever since the "outing" Rick had become much more, let's say, relaxed in his job. His enthusiasm for our sessions appeared to have waned a bit as grew visibly exhausted with the experience of working in a county mental health facility. I believed he know spent his days dreaming of a six-figure income at the hands of urban professionals with "issues." Not that I could blame him. I wouldn't want to be sentenced to listening to the problems of a bunch of crazy women - some suicidal, some homicidal, some both. The only difference between Rick and I as I saw it, was that he was sentenced to lead and I to follow.

I didn't have many "breakthroughs" in my therapeutic course, but the few I did have were big. One such event happened during group therapy where a shocked Rick looked as though he had just found the cure for cancer, AIDS and every other disease plaguing the universe. I was glad I could help.

The session began as they usually do, with Rick talking about trust or compassion or addiction or whatever. I still had not begun to participate very much in these sessions and viewed them solely as a source of entertainment - another episode of Days of Our Lives, if you will. But the morning after my session with Dr. Leslie and Michael found me still shaken by the knowledge that I just might be insane and I could not shake it. For the first time since I had arrived the Depakote did not stabilize my mood enough to warrant sleep and I spent the whole night wide awake remembering horrible episodes in my life. Some of which I felt the need to share, unprovoked, in group that morning. Although I thought it was provoked when Rick opened the floor to "sharing about our illness."

"I'll tell you what I'd like to share," I began. "I'd like to share the fact that I'm insane and that I have a history of being a horrible person."

"Um...OK, Carrie, what do..." Rick, shocked by my sudden willingness to talk, said. I cut him off.

"I mean, let's start at the beginning, shall we?" I said. "I have, from what I have been told, always been...manic. Or should we say, a maniac? I am prone to violent and unstable behavior. And I've thought about that. I've been thinking about that a lot and all I can say is, great, so what do I do now? I can't be expected to go back and live a normal life, can I? How can I be trusted to take care of my children if I'm prone to unstable behavior?

"I remember a few times when I wasn't exactly abusive to my children, but my temper certainly got the best of me. I smacked Jack once, hard. Right across the face. I don't remember why. He was whining about something or maybe having a tantrum and I smacked him. I left my handprint on his poor little cheek. Now what kind of mother does that? And Maddie I once wanted to throw across the room. I didn't, but I wanted to. Instead I sat her down, kind of hard, on the couch. But what if I was manic? What if I was out of control and I did throw her across the room?"

"Carrie," Rick said, "Your medications are designed to keep you from..."

"Oh, OK, so I just trust that this medication is going to work? What if I forget to take it? I forgot to take my birth control pills and now I have Maddie. The consequence of not taking my new medication is a bit more severe don't you think?"

I continued to rant for quite a while, putting Rick down at every turn. Until Valerie stepped in.

"So what are you saying Carrie? Are you saying you're going to stay here forever? That you'll never go home?"

"Well, I don't know. Maybe," I said, although I hadn't thought that's what I meant.

"So you're just going to hide here because you have this disease and never try your real life again?"

"I don't know."

"Do you love your kids?"

"Yes."

"Do you want to hurt them?"

"No, of course not, but that's not what I'm saying..."

"Then don't. It's as simple as that Carrie. If you love your kids then take your meds and don't hurt them. Stop bullshitting about it and get over it."

And there it was, my father's words coming to haunt me again. Get over it. But it wouldn't be that simple and as often as I'd thought I'd gotten over it, I would need to get over it again.

I was silent, stunned. Valerie had never spoken so harshly to me. I had often watched as others incurred her wrath, but I had never been on the receiving end. It stung. Not so much because I loved her so, but because she was right - although I didn't know that then. Right then I was pissed off that someone had said these things and that no one seemed to understand what I was feeling.

I sat back in my chair and sulked for the rest of the session. I half listened as Rhonda or Sheila or someone went on about their problems and how someone had done them wrong. I resolved to never speak of my feelings again, a typical response by me when someone dared to tell me the truth.

Rick pronounced the session over and came over to me.

"You really made excellent progress today, Carrie," he said. "You should be very proud of yourself and I am glad I was able to make you feel comfortable enough to release your emotions." He really said this, "release your emotions." He was beaming and I am sure he was now convinced that he was God's gift to psychiatry.

"Thanks," I mumbled and then worked my down the hall back to my room. I sat down on my bed and stared out the window. If this is what expressing yourself got you, I thought, than to hell with it. It wasn't worth it. I thought "releasing" my emotions about my illness was supposed to make me feel better. I felt worse. Much worse. And even though the meds still coursed through my system, I wasn't sure I wouldn't be better off dead. Now, could that be my disorder or could a person - even a person with a stabilized mood - just feel that way? I didn't know. I didn't seem to know anything anymore.

"You know," Valerie said as she opened my door, "I wasn't trying to hurt your feelings."

"Hmm…" I said, not looking up.

"I wasn't," she said and she sat down next to me on the bed. "I was just trying to make a point. I don't know. You've always been so great at listening and always seem so cool, maybe I just didn't want to think that you really do belong here."

"Thanks a lot."

"No, I mean, you're like, the most normal person I know - besides the not eating thing. You're such a…mom. I would give anything to have a mom like you - or be a mom like you."

It was then I realized how much my rant must have hurt Valerie. Valerie, who would give anything to have her baby back, and who would never have the chance to be a mother to that child.

"You know Val," I said, "You can still have other children."

"Yeah," she said and then she pulled away and stood up. "I know. But I don't want any other children. I want my baby."

"I know, I know," I said. "I'm sorry. I just meant…"

"No, I know what you meant," she said, sitting back down. "And, it's cool. Maybe I will have other babies, but not for a long time."

"I'm glad you haven't closed the door on that possibility."

"But I'm here to talk about you," she said. "Stop changing the subject. I didn't mean to hurt your feelings. You obviously love your kids. Isn't that enough for you? You've got a great husband and great kids. Just chill out."

"But what about everything…" I almost told her everything I had done, the money, the fraud, but I stopped myself.

"What? The money thing? Yes, I read about you in the newspaper - Fido left her copy in the showers. So what? It's just money, it's not worth killing yourself over."

"Yeah, but I hurt a lot of people," I said.

"So, a lot of people hurt a lot of people. Are you going to do it again?"

"No."

"Would you do it again if you knew then what you now?"

"I don't know."

"What do you mean?"

"I mean, I don't know," I said. "I mean, if we were struggling like that again and the power was off and I didn't have any food - I might do it, or something like it, again to take care of my family."

"Yeah," she said, "I see what you mean."

"So, I don't know. Yeah, I might. I'm horrible person."

"No, you're not. But you've got to stop this self-pity thing. Get over it, OK? Just do it. Go on. Yeah, you did a bad thing. You're paying for it aren't you? You didn't kill anybody. You took some money. Big deal. I used to take money out of my mother's purse, it didn't put me in here."

"It's hardly the same…"

"Yeah, but it's kind of the same. Just get past it. Tell them you won't do it anymore and move on - go be a mom. It's just money, Carrie, it's not worth dying over."

"You said that already," I said, smiling, trying to lighten up the mood.

"Yeah, well, I'm saying it again," she said and then she punched me in the shoulder. "Come on, let's go to lunch."

"Yeah, OK."

And for the first time in a long time, I felt…not bad. I wasn't happy, but I wasn't desperately sad either. It was just money. It wasn't worth killing myself over. I wish someone had said that to me earlier. Without knowing it, right there, right then, Valerie saved my life.

After lunch, I met with Dr. Leslie. We talked about my breakdown in group and Valerie. I told her how worried I was about being ill and how I didn't think I could be a good other again - if I ever was in the first place. I talked about Valerie and how she had put this whole thing - my crime, my illness - into perspective for me, but that I was still afraid. I was afraid of just being alive and ever having to go back out into the world and appear normal again.

"You don't have to appear normal," Dr. Leslie said. "You just have to be what's normal for you."

But I wasn't buying it. How could I ever fit in with people like Phyllis or Joan again and still be what I was, a crazy person? And then it occurred to me that I wouldn't be able to be with people like Phyllis again. They wouldn't want me to volunteer at the school anymore. They would shun me. My life would never be like it was. Insane or not, people would never believe I was anything but a criminal.

"People who know you and love you will accept you," Dr. Leslie said.

"There aren't that many people out there," I said.

I would have to move. Maybe to a whole different state, but I would have to survive at least two years under probation. Suddenly, the idea of ever leaving the institution became very unappealing. People would have seen me in the paper. People would know who I was. How could I ever give my kids of a normal life if I couldn't even go to the store?

"Believe me, Carrie, people have much more going on in their lives than recognizing you at the supermarket," Dr. Leslie said.

"Yeah, I guess," I said.

But the problem continued to gnaw at me even after the session. Dr. Leslie said it was "progress" that I recognized my illness, now it was just a matter of making it fit into my life. It's strange, when I didn't believe I was ill, I wanted to leave, now that I know what's wrong with me and know that it can be fixed (well, sort of) with medication, I want to stay. I don't want to face any of it.

Chapter 15:

Michael brought my camera at one visit. He said he had cleared it with Dr. Leslie and they thought it would be a good idea. Something familiar for me and something for me to do.

"You need to get back into your life," Michael said.

I nodded my head as I ran my hands over the camera and pretended to adjust the lens. Didn't they know that this camera represented everything that I did wrong? I had no desire to take pictures again. No desire to try and make a living at it.

"What if I don't want my old life back?" I asked.

"Well, then you have to decide that don't you?" he replied. We sat quiet for a minute, maybe more. And then I asked him something I had been wanting to ask for a long time, but couldn't.

"Did you know I was crazy all these years?" I asked. Michael took a deep breath and thought for a minute.

"I mean," I continued, "did it ever cross your mind that I was really insane?"

"Well, no," he said. "I guess your, um, enthusiasm, is what I always loved about you, but sometimes...a couple of times in particular, I wondered if there was something wrong. I mean, you have a good temper on you, but a lot of people do, but…" He got quiet again. But I knew the times he was talking about. Michael and I have always had good arguments, but they were never physical or even particularly mean, except for the time I threw the bowl and another time, after I had Maddie. That time I freaked out again. I was angry that Michael hadn't called me one night. He was very late and had gone out with some guys from work. I sat up all night, worrying, waiting for the phone to ring, waiting for a police officer to come to the door and tell me my husband died in a car accident. I sat on the couch all night wondering what I would do if Michael died. I even thought about his funeral and how I would tell his family. When he finally came home, all of the sadness and anger raged up inside me again and I hit him, just like the time I had found my high school boyfriend in the Kentucky Fired Chicken. Michael, who was a bit drunk at the time, took me by the arms and tried to get me to stop. When I wouldn't, he backhanded me across the face and I landed on the couch. I curled up there and stared off into space. I didn't speak to him for a week.

Michael felt horrible. I knew he did. He spent that week doing more dishes and laundry than I had ever seen him do before. He apologized over and over again. Michael was not a violent person. I had never heard him raise his voice to the children, much less spank them and even during our arguments, he rarely yelled. I wasn't worried that he had suddenly turned into a wife-beater, but I was going to make him pay for what he had done. I did not take into account at all what I had done. I held myself completely blameless, even though I left bruises all over Michael's arms.

"I'm sorry," I said, crying. "I don't even know what to say. You should just leave me and go find a normal person."

"You're forgiven," Michael said. "And I won't lie to you, I've thought a lot about leaving you over these last five months. And, I don't know. I can't predict the future. I don't know if we'll be able to make it through this, but I do love you. I keep coming back to that fact. I love you, no one else and I want this to work. Besides, no one else makes life nearly as exciting as you do." He put his arms around me and I cried long and hard, but the first time in a long time I didn't feel alone. I knew Michael couldn't promise to stay forever. I was shocked he was even considering it, but he was here now and that was good enough.

After Michael left, I looked over my camera again. He had left me some film and I loaded it, but then put the camera back in its case. I wasn't sure what to think of it just yet.

Life on the second floor got a little more exciting with the addition of a new face. We had new faces on the ward all of the time, of course, but most of them were just temporary. Women undergoing psychiatric evaluations before a trial or drying out after a night on the town. But Jill was there to stay, at least for a while. They brought her in very drunk one night and put her in an isolation room to dry her out. She woke up late the next day, after the rest of us had already had group, and spent the better part of an hour in the shower.

The rest of us, assembled in our near-permanent positions on the sofa in the lounge in front of the soaps, watched her as she moved from the shower to her new room, changing her clothes and fixing her hair. She had her own pajamas, silk ones, that she had apparently arranged to bring along. When she was done, she went over to the soda machine and put a dollar in.

"Goddamnit!" We heard her yell. "Am I to understand that the only drinks in this machine are caffeine free?" Lacking anything better to do, I got up and walked over to her.

"I know," I said, "it sucks doesn't it? But caffeine can interact with your meds, so it's a caffeine-free existence."

"What?" she turned and looked at me as though I was a piece of gum she had just scraped off her shoe.

"The caffeine - it mixes with the medication," I said, suddenly feeling like that piece of gum.

"Oh," she said. "Sorry. OK. You wouldn't have a cigarette would you?"

"That I do have," I said. "Come on, I'll show you the smoke room."

"God, there's a room for that too?"

"Yup," I said. "I think you'll find we have a whole range of amenities here at Crazy Woman East." She smiled and followed me down to the smoke room. We sat on the card table and lit the first of many cigarettes. One of the volunteers posted outside the nearby isolation gave us our first lights and then I illustrated my now expert lighting one cigarette off another technique.

"So," I said, "what are you in for?"

"They tell me I'm an alcoholic and an addict and that I tried to jump off a building a few weeks ago," she said, quite nonchalantly. "I was in a private hospital for a while, but I left quite without permission and went out to have a drink. I got into a fight with a bitchy bartender and the police brought me here, but I don't think I'll be staying for long."

"Oh, but, why aren't you still in isolation?"

"Because I told them that if they didn't let me out of that pissy little room I was going to call the governor and have them all fired."

"And you would be in a position to do that?"

"Yes," she said in a way that made me not want to pursue it further.

With that, we stubbed out our cigarettes and I showed her around the floor. I went to my room to put away the book I had been carrying around all morning, but had yet to crack, before lunch, when I heard yelling at the nurses' station. Jill was making it known that she would not be forced to eat with a bunch of crazies and that she would not be treated like these "people." She then demanded to see her lawyer and said she would wait for her tray in her room.

For once, even Nurse McKinley looked like she didn't know what to do next. The rest of the girls on the floor watched from the lounge. It was better than Days of Our Lives. Instinctively, I grabbed my camera and, from behind a large column in the hallway that divided the hall from the lounge, took pictures of the girls looking at the nurses. Then I took pictures of the nurses frantically making phone calls and demanding that a tray be brought up to the second floor. No one, since Valerie, had ever thrown so much chaos into the second floor and even Valerie hadn't made such an impact on Nurse McKinley.

After the commotion died down and Nurse McLaughlin had told the rest of us to please line up for lunch did I notice the camera in my hand. I carefully put it away, still a little surprised by its presence, and followed the line down the hall.

At lunch, the table was buzzing with news of the new girl.

"I heard she's the daughter of some famous actor," Sheila said.

"No, no, she's like the heir to some fortune - a big company," Rhonda added.

I sat and listened to their banter. I almost contributed my own findings, but decided to keep quiet. It was odd for the table to be this active without Valerie's presence. Valerie had been in a special session for hours. She did not make group that morning and she was still missing when lunch wrapped up. I asked Nurse McLaughlin about her, but I didn't get a response. She just told me to keep eating and not worry about her.

Valerie did show up later in the day, while we were having our "outside time." Jill had also decided to join us and spent the hour filing her nails and smoking, captivating the other girls with tails from bars and men she had dated. Valerie just sat in the grass and stared off into space.

"Hey," I said. "What's up?"

"My mother's dead," she said.

"Oh my God, Valerie. I'm so sorry."

"Yeah, me too."

"Do you know how...?" I asked.

"Yeah. The fucking bastard did it. He was beating her, she called the police, he shot her, tried to shoot the police and then they shot him. End of story."

"Jesus."

"Yeah. You know, she wasn't a great mother, but...I don't know, she had her moments. And I think she loved me." A tear rolled down Val's cheek, something I had never seen before, not even when she talked about her baby. I tried to put my arm around her and think of something profound to say, but I couldn't. She pushed my arm away.

"I gotta go."

"OK," I said, "Where do you want to go?"

"No, I mean, I gotta get out of this place. It's time for me to go."

"Do you think that's such a good idea? Maybe you should stay for a bit, try and work this out in your head before you go."

"My head is worked out fine. I can't be here anymore. I don't want to talk about my mother or my baby or my stepfather anymore. I'm done."

"Where will you go?"

"I don't know. Chicago maybe. Or California. I've always wanted to go there. I need a new life. I'm sick of this place, this town. I've been here too long already."

"OK," I said. It seemed like the only thing to say. I wasn't going to convince her to stay. She had that look in her eyes, an unapproachable, completely resolved glaze that told me not to pursue it any further.

"OK," she said.

After our conversation, Valerie didn't linger. It was almost as if she was seeking my permission to go. I prayed for the first time in a very long time while I watched her pack her backpack. I prayed that she wouldn't go walk into traffic or leap off a building. I wanted Valerie to make it. Of all the people, me included, who deserved to go out and find a good life, it was Valerie. I wanted to tell her that. I wanted to let her know that she could always write me or call me and I would do anything I could to help her. But I knew she wouldn't take my help. She would go out and do it on her own - and either she would fail spectacularly, or she would succeed, spectacularly.

She hugged everyone one the ward goodbye. Rhonda and Sheila and everyone else who had clung to Valerie's sweatshirts for so long, cried. Wailed would actually be a more appropriate word. Sheila got down on the floor and begged her not to leave. Valerie patted her on the head, softly and then hugged Nurse McLaughlin and even shook Nurse McKinley's hand. Jill watched from the lounge, filing her nails, uncomprehending of the light that was leaving the ward.

Valerie walked over to me. This was my moment, I thought, to tell her everything. But she just looked me in the eye, squeezed my hand and walked down the hall. She didn't look back once, but pushed open the heavy door as it buzzed and was gone. I felt like with that one hand squeeze, I had conveyed everything I had hoped for her. I hope she felt it too.

No one talked much after Valerie left. Sheila continued to wail until Nurse McKinley sedated her and took her to her room. I stood in the lounge for a while, but the atmosphere was vastly different. It felt as though someone had taken a vacuum to the room and sucked all of the life out of it. I walked back to room and sat on my bed. I opened my journal and for the first time since I had arrived, I wrote. Mostly I wrote about Valerie and what I hoped her life would become, but as time went on I wrote about me and Michael and what I hoped my own life would become.

For the first time since I had become a permanent resident of the ward, I didn't want to stay. My heart was heavy with Valerie's departure but it was also, mildly, buoyant at the prospect of leaving. It was almost as if Valerie's leaving gave me permission to want to leave. Now, I just had to figure out what to do with myself in the meantime. And what to do once I got out. Just because I now felt like leaving, it didn't mean that I wouldn't face a million problems once I left.

Tired of my own thoughts, I wandered back out into the lounge before dinner. Things seemed to be getting back to normal, so to speak, since Valerie left. The wailing had stopped, the meds had been dispensed and the TV was back on. Jill, I noticed, was either still filing her nails nearly two hours after Valerie's goodbyes or had just returned to what was now her seat. I walked over and sat down next to her. She looked up up at me briefly and then absently went back to the filing. Only, as I looked down at her hands, there was so filing to be done. She filed her nails down past the quick and was now eating into her skin - causing it to bleed on some fingers.

"Jesus," I whispered, not wanting to call attention to her. "What are you doing?" I pulled the emery board from her hand.

"What?" She said. "I'm just trying to get them off. This is the only thing that works." Even more frightening than her behavior was the fact that she was so calm about it.

"Christ, just…hang on a minute," I said, scanning the room for an appropriate authority. Nurse McKinley was around, but I didn't want her to make a huge deal out of it. She wasn't exactly Nurse Ratchett, but she could sure embarrass the hell out of you when you did something…crazy. Nurse McLaughlin was gone for the night, so I grabbed a junior nurse who had worked in the institution longer than anyone. I thought her name was Carol. She was very short and very fat, but moved quicker than I had ever seen the lithe Nurse McKinley move when I told her what Jill was doing.

Carol obviously suspected something, but I did not know what. She deftly gathered Jill up and ushered her to the medical examination room. Soon after, a psychiatrist (not Dr.Leslie), the head medical doctor (who I recognized from the hospital ward after my stabbing) and Nurse McKinley all filed sternly into the exam room. Jill quietly came out as they went in. Carol wandered back to the nurses' station and picked up some other work, but she seemed distracted. I wanted to know what was up with Jill but we were never allowed to ask. We had to get our information through eavesdropping or, occasionally, someone would tell us. I didn't know Carol well, she rotated weekly from floor to floor - kind of a nursing Jack of All Trades - but she looked just disturbed enough that she might tell me something. I feigned trouble with the soda machine and when she came over to help, I asked her what was up with Jill.

"She's just exhibiting some signs of the DT's," she said. "Delirium tremens, which isn't unusual. But what is unusual is that it means she was probably drinking recently - here - and we have to find out where and how."

"Oh," I said. "Is there anything I can do to help?" Suddenly I felt very responsible for Jill's care.

"No, no," she said. "They've got it covered now. You did great, getting me when you did. Here's your soda."

"Thanks," I said.

"No problem," and just like that, she went back to work. Just another day on the job for Carol.

Chapter 16:

While Jill was gone, wherever they had taken her to detox again, I had a visitor.

My mother had never visited me at the hospital before. And I didn't blame her for not coming, although it did seem a little strange that I could be there for almost nine months and not get a visit. After all, Michael had brought the children on their birthdays and every other Sunday and he came every week. But not one visit from my mother. First, she was busying cleaning my house and taking care of my children. Second, it was weird. My mother and I were not really close in a mother-daughter sense. I mean, I loved her and she loved me, but if we weren't related I don't think we would choose to hang out together. It was nothing I could put my finger on. We had never really fought that much, but we just weren't alike in any way I could see. I called every Sunday to check in, but, when I was not in a mental hospital, we saw each other rarely. Even though I only lived three hours away, we only got together for the kids' birthdays, Thanksgiving and Christmas.

Frankly, my parents were boring. Once the present opening and feast eating was done, there was nothing left to talk about. Michael and my father always found work stuff to talk about - or power tools, and my mother and I talked about Maddie and Jack, but that was it. We had no common interests, no funny stories to share. If the kids and Michael weren't around, it would be very much like the dinners I had as a child. Very quiet. I was an only child and dinners were silent affairs. Even when we talked, it was silent. I loved going over to my best friend Julie's house back then. She had four brothers and dinners were raucous affairs filled with laughing and yelling. There was always an argument about something or a funny story from school. Julie on the other hand, loved my house because I had everything to my self and there was no one to fight with. I imagine the constant quiet was welcome to her, but to me, it was oppressive.

Julie was the daughter my mother always wanted. They got along easily and talked quietly in the kitchen about projects in home economics class and different boys. It was a rapport I had never developed with my mother - or anyone but Julie for that matter. But Julie had a natural knack for that. She could become friends, almost instantaneously with almost anyone. There was no one in all of St. Elizabeth's who didn't know her and like her. Her name was always in the paper and she was forever being waved to when we walked through town after school. I had lived in St. Elizabeth's all my life and didn't know half the people Julie did.

I stared at my mother for a minute or so through the visiting door's window before going in. She was obviously nervous, pulling at her hands and then rubbing her palms on her thighs over and over. I took a deep breath and then walked in with a big smile on my face.

"Hi Mom," I said. "How are you?"

"Good, good," she said, rising to hug me. "How are you?"

"Oh, you know, I've been better," I said, hugging her lightly.

"Sure, sure," she said, sitting back down. My mother repeated everything. It was one of my biggest pet peeves. Everything is "good, good," or "fine, fine."

"Well," I said, "how are the kids? They're not giving you too much trouble are they?"

"Oh, not at all, not at all," she said.

"Good, good," I said. Now I was doing it, lovely. Let's get this off on the right foot, I thought. "I can't tell you how much I appreciate everything you've done. And I'm so sorry for all the trouble." Then tears started to well up in my eyes. This had been happening a lot lately. Every time I even ventured an apology or to even think about my illness and my crime, I cried. And I couldn't stop it. I can feel the lump forming even now as I write this, years later.

"Oh, no, don't be sorry," she said. "Well, be sorry for what you did, but don't be sorry for being sick. You didn't know."

"But..."

"No, no. That's not why I'm here. I'm here because I want to talk to you about your father."

"Daddy? Is he OK?" My father and I had always gotten along great. We were buddies, going to ballgames and farm auctions together when I was little and even a few when I was a teenager. But my father was also very harsh. He expected a lot of me, which is why I wasn't surprised that he wouldn't lend me money when I called him. He didn't believe in lending money - not to a friend or even a daughter. "A man has to make his own way in this world," he always said. He could also get ferociously angry. I don't remember him ever hitting me or my mother, but he could be silent for days if one of us made him angry. He would go to his den - the only room in the house we weren't allowed in, unless my mother was going to clean it - and stay there until bedtime, while my mother and I watched TV, silently, in the living room.

"Daddy's fine," she said. "But, and I don't know why I never mentioned it sooner, but, well, he has, I think, the same illness as you."

"What?"

"Bipolar disorder, manic depression, I'm not sure which, but one of them," she said.

"They're the same thing, Mom," I said.

"Oh, OK, then that. He has that. We didn't know about it until a few years ago. I took a survey for him in a Good Housekeeping magazine about depression and at the end it said he should go see a doctor. And for some reason, he did. Just made an appointment and went. Anyway, he's been on something, Lithium, ever since. We didn't think to tell you."

"What?" I yelled. My mother was frightened by my sudden outburst. "What? My father's been on Lithium - an anti-psychotic drug - for a few years and you didn't think to tell me?"

"Calm down, Carrie," she said. "Sit down. Why do you think I'm here now? I'm just saying, it's quite possible this thing you have is related."

"Um, yes, Mom, I'd say that was very likely."

"Well, then," she said. "Good. Now you know." She seemed so pleased with herself. I hated that about my mother. She would stay silent and stay silent and then just come out with some little piece of information - anything - and just insert it into a conversation, subsequently killing the conversation. She used to do this at dinner. My father and I might finally start talking about something, maybe a girl who bugged me at school and Mom wouldn't participate at all for the longest time, but then, usually right after I called the girl at school a puke-face or something, she would say in a whisper, "Her mother has cancer." And then, appearing to be pleased with herself for stopping the conversation completely, would resume eating. She was very weird, my mother.

"Well," she said. "I should get back. I have some errands to run." Was I just another errand on the list? I wondered. Get milk and bread, stop at drycleaners, tell Carrie her father's on Lithium, pick up Jack from school.

I rose to hug her.

"Thanks, Mom," I said. "For everything. I really appreciate everything you're doing."

"I know," she said. "Just get better. We're all praying for you."

The usual anger toward my mother subsided as my guilt returned. She was a good mother, better than me, certainly. And she hadn't cast me out of the family. She was just, well, kooky. She also did come to see me - however bizarre the experience was.

I sat back down on the tweed couch, thinking about my father. It certainly explained a lot, but I couldn't think of any way to blame him. I wanted what I did to be someone's fault...someone else's fault...but I couldn't make it happen. If anything, the knowledge that my father had the same disease and yet somehow escaped doing anything criminal - did, in fact, lead a completely normal façade of a life - made it worse. I now not only felt criminal and manic-depressive, but weak too.

Jill came back to us several days later and finally started to get into the routine. I still hadn't figured out who she was that she could snap her fingers and get the staff in motion, but I had it down to either the daughter of a major CEO or the daughter of an important politician.

Her first day back, she was instructed to attend group with the rest of us.

"What's that like?" she asked. "Is it really touchy, feely and all that?"

"No," I said. "It's not too bad. Rick isn't like a group hugger or anything, but he does sound idiotic most of the time. Most of the session is spent trying to get one girl or another to 'release her emotions,' and today it will probably be you."

"Oh my God," she said.

"No, don't worry. Just nod and smile a lot, like you know exactly what he means and he'll think he's made a breakthrough. Building up his ego is essential to getting out of doing any real releasing."

"All right, good to know."

We walked into group together and as promised, Rick made a big fuss over our new groupee. I smiled and nodded my way through the session, encouraging both Rick and Jill who seemed to be made for each other - each needing a variety of verbal pats on the back in order to get through the session. Their conversations during group went something like:

"Jill, thank you so much for coming to us today," Rick said. "You have shown a lot of courage in coming here to share your feelings."

"Thanks Rick," Jill said, "I am happy to be here and begin my recovery and get through this chapter in my life. From what I've heard here today, you will be very helpful in leading me - and the other girls - to the other side."

Then Rick would beam, secure in the knowledge that he was righting the world's wrongs and Jill would beam because she had so successfully snowed him. They were going to get along just fine - I just wondered whether or not Jill would actually recover from anything.

I expressed this concern at my next meeting with Dr. Leslie.

"That's fine," she said, "but you need to let Jill worry about her recovery. You need to worry about your own."

"I know, but, I don't know," I said. "I guess I'm worried about her."

"It must be hard for you, now that Valerie is gone," she said. "But you can't supplant your worry over Valerie on someone new. Jill needs to take care of Jill, Valerie needs to take care of Valerie and you need to take care of Carrie.

"Besides, it's time to begin designing your plan for reentering your life."

"What?"

"You've been here over nine months, Carrie," she said. "And you are going to be leaving us soon. We need to think about how you are going to cope once you leave."

I was silent.

"I see here you've been taking some classes downstairs in the arts center," she continued. "Have the pottery classes been fun?"

"It's something to do," I muttered.

"And I have a note here that says you requested permission to use the photo lab just the other day…"

"I had some pictures to develop," I said.

"Did they turn out?"

"They're OK," I said. What I didn't say was that they were actually quite good. They were a series of black and whites I had been taking of the women on the second floor and the other patients out in the courtyard. Some of them I under-exposed, so the faces were dark, but the body and the place were obvious. It had taken me a while to figure out how to do it, but it was worth it. I had random thoughts of publishing the photos one day, but was hung up on two distinct thoughts - how could I ever try and make a living at photography again considering all I had done? And, who would be interested in a bunch of pictures of mental patients?

As my departure date neared, my nighttime anxiety attacks increased. It was almost humorous, I told Dr. Leslie. The first nine - or was it ten - months crawled by, each day an insurmountable obstacle. When I woke up each morning, I sighed, not ready to face another interminable day in that place. But as ninety days left became sixty and eventually thirty, I couldn't find enough hours in the day. There were still pictures I wanted to take, the camera becoming an obsession for me that it had never been before. I felt safe behind it. Rather than just a tool for making money or something that I was reasonably good at, it became an extension of my arm. It was no longer the camera and what it represented that I feared, but what was behind it - me - and the camera was a good way to hide. Not that I knew any of this then. All I knew then was that I had a manic desire to take pictures.

There were also many other activities filling my days. I was a regular in the art department and had many craft projects going on at once. It makes me laugh now, to know that I was becoming manic again - but because my mania was manifesting itself in more "socially acceptable" ways, not even Dr. Leslie recognized it. I was getting better they all said. I was participating in activities. I was reintegrating myself into the real world. Basically, I was using my illness for good instead of evil.

I filled each day with minutiae Lists for when I got home - jobs I thought I could do, things to do with Jack and Maddie to make up for the lost time, things to do for Michael, home improvement projects. You name it, I had a list for it in those last weeks.

A list for jobs went something like this:

1. Flower shop. Pros: like flowers, no criminal background check. Cons: Daytime hours, miss time with kids.

2. School bus driver. Pros: Can bring Maddie and be home for Jack afterschool. Cons: Possible criminal background check, hate driving.

3. Nursing Assistant. Pros: Good money, helping people, day care offered for Maddie. Cons: Have to take classes, criminal background check.

4. Waitress. Pros: Decent money, no background check. Cons: Night hours.

And so on. What hit me the hardest with this list was that for the rest of my life, or at least, for the next seven years, I would have a criminal record. Even if it was a misdemeanor, I would still come up on a check. And, in addition to my now extremely bad credit, this would be yet another thing for people to judge me on.

I also seriously considered nursing school. I stayed up at night and thought about how such a job, where I would have to help others and be unselfish for once. I thought it was the perfect solution. A good paying job that would wear me out and make me put others problems before my own. I asked for, and received, permission to use the Internet in the hospital "library"

- a tribute to my recent good behavior. I researched what was involved extensively and even downloaded the application to the local tech school, but as I read about what was involved, I became convinced that with my record no one would let me be a nurse. Even if I could pass the required chemistry classes - a feat in itself - I would have to beg the registry board to take me on because of my history.

"I mean, how fucked up is that?" I asked Dr. Leslie during my session.

"Calm down," she said. "Just what is so fucked up about it? The people in charge have to make sure that the people they register are not going to harm or take advantage of their patients. If nursing is really what you want to do, then you'll be committed enough to convince a board that you're better and not a danger to patients."

"It's still fucked up," I said. "Look at this list. Half of the jobs on it will do some sort of background check - even if I just want to drive a Goddamned Frito Lay truck. I'll never get a job."

"I don't think that's true," she said. "I think that's an easy excuse for you not to try. But let's be real. For a while, you might not be able to do things that could endanger others. They need to do background checks. You wouldn't want Jack's bus driver to be a released child molester would you?"

"I would hardly equate me with a child molester."

"Let's be honest, Carrie. You are never going to get a job as a bank teller, but I see no reason why you couldn't be a nurse eventually or a teacher or even a photographer again - as long as you're not in charge of the money."

"Is that some sort of lame joke?"

"Well, I hoped it would make you smile, but no. It's the truth. And while we're talking honestly, tell me, what's the real issue here? Is it the fact that you're afraid you'll be turned down for these jobs? Or, maybe, is it that you're embarrassed people will find out about your past at all?"

"No," I said. "Yes. Both."

"OK, then. Let me ask you something else. Why are you in such a hurry to find yourself a new career? I think you need some time just to readjust to your life, not start a whole new one."

"But I want a new one."

"I know. And you'll have it, but you'll need to get back into your old life first."

"Yeah."

"I'm going to assemble a list of counselors that you can see once you leave as well as a couple of support groups that will be immensely helpful to you. In addition, you should attend the meetings Michael has been going to. It will give you some idea of what he has been going through over the last year and will help you identify with him more. Next time, we need to get into how you and Michael are going to start living with each other again. A year is a long time to be apart and you need to prepare yourself for being married again."

"Michael's meeting?"

"Yes. I'm sorry, I thought he told you. He's been going to a group we have downtown for the friends and family of the mentally ill."

"Oh." No one had ever called me mentally ill before. I mean, I knew I had a mental illness, but being one of the mentally ill was a whole different thing. I just kind of looked at myself as a regular person who needed medication, but hearing her say that - friends and family of the mentally ill - shot through me. Michael was the spouse of a mentally ill person. Jack and Maddie had a mentally unstable mother. Mentally ill. Back in my room, I said it over and over to myself in the mirror, watching the words form on my lips.

"You are mentally ill, Carrie."

"Ms. O'Connor, you are one of the mentally ill."

"I am mentally ill."

I splashed some water on my face and then looked up at my reflection. I watched the water drip from my lips as I said "mentally ill." It was unnerving. But at the same time, the words started to lose their meaning, kind of like when you're young and you wonder why a chair is called a chair and a desk a desk and not the other way around.

I spent lunch and group that afternoon looking at myself from outside. I was conscious of each step I took wondering with both fascination and a degree of disgust at how I came to be me. Each word out of my mouth or movement of my hand surprised me to no end. I sat through group, silent, yet telling my brain to move a finger or a toe. I remembered thinking these thoughts as a child, in my pre-mentally ill stage, as I had come to think of it. Why was I me? Why did I have this illness? This life? But for the first time in years, instead of dwelling on it and feeling sorry for myself because of it I didn't wonder how to change it, I wondered how I could accept it.

Chapter 17:

hy didn't you tell me you were going to a support group?" I asked Michael at his next visit…just three weeks from my release.

"I don't know," he said, sorting Maddie out with a coloring book. We were in the same old visitation room. With the same old tweed sofa and chairs. Jack was playing with a remote control truck I - meaning my mother - had gotten him for his birthday just last week. I missed my child's seventh birthday. The first one ever. I felt wretched over it. I should have felt more terrible over the last one - a big bash I threw for him and his friends from school, courtesy of my accounting skills. I justified the expenditures then as what any mother would do for her child and still felt more horrible over the fact that I couldn't throw him another party than over what I had done to give it to him. He didn't seem to mind, though, running around the room with his $10 remote control truck.

"What do you mean you don't know?" I asked, trying to be light. "I was just surprised, that's all. I'm glad you found a group. Does it help? Are they nice?"

"Of course they're nice Carrie," he said. "It's a support group. They just talk about their families and friends who have problems and how they deal with it. I don't talk a lot."

"But you do talk a little?"

"Sometimes."

"What do you say?"

"Does it really matter Carrie?" He sighed. "Do we have to talk about this now?"

"Yes," I said. "Don't get upset. I think it's important. I want to know what's bothering you - well, I mean, the most. What bothers you the most?"

"God, I don't know," he said. "Sometimes I just get frustrated with trying to do it all alone."

"But you're not alone, not really," I said, getting a little defensive. "You have your parents and my parents and Emily said she tries to help."

"It's not exactly the same," he said.

"I know. But…"

"Look, it's just hard, OK? I miss you all of the time, but then sometimes I don't. I worry about how it's going to be when you're back and I wonder if I can handle it all."

"Handle what all?"

"Taking care of you and the kids."

"I can take care of myself just fine, thank you."

"No, apparently you can't." Ouch. That hurt. And it was true. I didn't know how I would take care of myself and the children, but it hadn't occurred to me that I wasn't the only one who thought this.

"Well, maybe I shouldn't come home," I said. My heart leapt into my throat and my stomach turned as I said this. I wanted him to say "No, of course not, come home, we love you." And I wanted him to mean it. He was silent for a minute. Too long. What if he agreed with me? What if he didn't want me back? I couldn't blame him. I was horrible and I was sure he had gotten used to living without me, but still...

"Carrie, that's not the answer," he said. I was briefly relieved. "Although don't think the idea hasn't occurred to me."

Ouch again.

"So?" I whispered. "What would you like me to do?"

"Just come home," he said. "We'll take it a step at a time."

"OK," I said. I sat quietly for the remainder of the visit, smiling at Jack and admiring Maddie's many pictures.

Michael kissed me on the head, like a child, as he left and for the first time I wondered not what it would be like to be dead or what it would be like when I went home, but what it would be like to be out on my own.

I had spent so much energy over the last year working on my problems and pitying myself that I rarely thought about the toll this was taking on Michael. He was the one who had to deal with our old friends and the knowledge that everyone in town had seen me in the paper. He had to go to work everyday and take the kids back to the school I had defrauded. He had to get up everyday and face the music, my music. He didn't have the concrete block façade of the mental institution to hide behind. He didn't have a mental illness to hide behind, as I did. He had to cope with everything I had done on the frontline, with no psychiatrist to support him. It's no wonder he went to a support group.

How were we going to be able to come together after so long apart? It's not like I was on an extended trip. I left him - albeit involuntary - in a lurch, with bills to pay and children to take care of. In fact, I had gotten the better part of the deal, it seemed. I had been whisked away, under the guise of being punished, to a place where I could hide behind my Camels and my medications. Michael had to bear the brunt of the punishment. It would have been more of a punishment if they hadn't sent me here at all.

I was back in Dr. Leslie's office trying to explain this theory to her. She wasn't buying it.

"How would it be better for you to be out there, facing the music, as you say, instead of here?"

"Well, I don't know, but it's more fair then having Michael out there fighting my battles for me," I said.

"He's not fighting your battles, Carrie," she said. "He's fighting his own. You keep making the mistake of putting your issues front and center. Certainly Michael's problems intertwine with yours, your married, they should. But your problems are your own. You have to solve them Michael is dealing with your family's problems, his problems, most likely the children's problems, but not yours."

"Yeah," I said.

"I'm serious now. You have to take yourself out of the equation. You are the one who will have to face these people head on when you go home. You are the one whose picture was in the paper. Not Michael. But you have to decide whether or not you are going to continue to hide or if you're going to go out there and make something of your life. What do you think, really, would have happened if you had stayed home instead of coming here?"

"I don't know."

"Yes, you do," she said. I was getting angry now. God she pissed me off sometimes. I leapt up from the cat hair-covered couch.

"I'd be dead, OK?" I screamed. "I'd be dead! And I'd be better off too!" Then I sat down and cried, again. What was funny about my crying this time was I didn't feel like I meant it. The tears came, but they almost felt forced and I had yelled, not because I felt like I'd be better off dead, but because it was a stupid, futile attempt for Dr. Leslie to keep me longer. If I was still suicidal, they couldn't send me home.

Unfortunately, Dr. Leslie knew this.

My nerves were on edge for my last weeks and then days at the institution. I went to endless meetings: group, sessions with Dr. Leslie, sessions with my new psychiatrist who would see me on the outside, meetings with my probation officer, meetings with my new "mentor" who would advise me on financial matters and take me out bowling once a week - kind of a big sister for the mentally ill.

It was endless. I had to sign papers right and left waiving this and acquiescing to that. I had to sign up for parenting classes and a new support group. I had to commit to some type of community service. I picked stocking food at the local food pantry.

I didn't have time to be nervous and I relished my allotted hour in front of the TV with the other girls during Days of Our Lives. I looked forward to a few minutes in the smoke room alone. And even though I still ate and showered with the other girls, I was already starting to feel like an outsider again. I was going home. They were not. At least, not anytime soon. Rhonda was a lifer, as was Sheila. Valerie was gone and we hadn't heard from her. Jill was still there, but she'd leave in a month or two and be on to her next binge.

So it was that on a Tuesday morning, one year and one week exactly, having recently looked at a calendar, since I had been admitted, that I was packed and sitting on my bed - in the clothes I had worn in - waiting for Michael to pick me up.

I said goodbye to everyone, each nurse and patient giving me a hug and wishing me luck. Even Janet got out of bed to say goodbye. I was sad, but I did not cry. I was happy to be leaving, to begin my life again, but sad to leave this comfortable place. This place where I felt I belonged and I was scared at what awaited me in the world again. I missed Valerie and asked Jill to write me and let me know how she was doing. Nurse McLaughlin walked me downstairs where Michael was signing my paperwork. He hugged me tightly, kissed me on the head and picked up my bag filled with letters and pictures from the children and the occasional letter from Michael or Emily.

Gandhi was a Libra

It was strange to ride in our old minivan, up and down the familiar streets that now seemed new. I noticed new houses and new stores - things had changed while I was inside, but for the most part they were the same. When we went on our trips with Rick, I hadn't noticed them, but now that I was coming back to this world, I saw everything clearly.

Pulling into our driveway, I saw my mother's car, my in-laws', Emily's. Michael squeezed my arm gently as I walked into the house. A Welcome Home Mommy banner hung above the kitchen. The kids ran to me and wouldn't let me go. Completely shocked, I hugged everyone. How could they be so happy to see me? How could they want me back again?

"We are so happy to see you," Emily said. "We missed you so much. Are you OK?"

"Hi," I said, stunned. "Yeah, I'm fine, I guess. What are you doing here?"

"What do you mean? You've been gone forever," she said and then she hugged me again and whispered in my ear, "We wanted you to know that we love you."

Tears welled up in my eyes. I couldn't believe my good fortune at having so many people still love me. The road ahead didn't look nearly as bleak.

I put the kids to bed for the first time in a year that night. I read them story after story and let them stay up way too late. I promised Jack he could skip school the next day so that we could do something special together. I relished helping them put on their pajamas and brush their teeth, chores I used to try and pawn off on Michael. How could I have ever wanted to leave them? Anything - the embarrassment, the humiliation, the hatred people had for me was worth enduring if it meant I could do this with my children, if it meant I would see them graduate and have their own children. One day, I thought, I'll just be crazy Grandma - nothing more.

I cleaned up after the impromptu party, watching myself wipe the counters and pick up paper plates. I unpacked my bag. It didn't take long. I placed the letters and pictures in a shoebox in my office. I lingered for a while in my office, almost completely untouched since I left. I looked at the rolls of film, piles of reprints, my portfolio and then I shut my eyes tight, hoping to block out the rest of the memories. Michael watched everything I did. I pretended not to notice. I wasn't sure if he was waiting for me to do something crazy or not. I pulled my new pill bottles out of my bag and lined them up on a shelf above the sink. I turned each of their labels out and placed them in order of when I needed to take them. Then I turned around and faced Michael.

"Worried I'm going to flip out or something?" I asked, smiling.

"No," he said. "I just missed having you around."

"Sure," I said, "you think that now, but soon you'll be wishing you had your freedom back." He pulled me to him and looked me in the eyes - a powerful gaze I hadn't held since we dated.

"No," he said. "I won't." And then, for the first time in a long time - even before I left - we ascended the stairs together and slept in our bed as one.

Chapter 18:

I spend two weeks almost entirely inside the house. When I do go out to shop or take Jack and Maddie to a park, I go at least ten miles out of town so that I can avoid run-ins with any former clients. Michael has been kind enough to continue to take Jack and Maddie to school, but I am dreading open houses and parent-teacher conferences, events I used to love.

I begin to consider moving far away, somewhere where we can get a fresh start. A farm maybe, in Montana - or Alaska. I watch a National Geographic special about several families that live in small cabins and lead self-sufficient lifestyles. We could do that, I think. I could bake bread and Michael could hunt for moose. We could raise the children alone and be together all of the time. Best of all, we wouldn't have to deal with people or spend our time earning money.

I talk about this newfound desire to escape at my first group session. My desire to run and hide is not unique.

"I wanted to do the same thing," one woman, Donna, said. "But not Alaska, no way. I wanted to live simply in like, Bali. Somewhere warm."

Everyone else in the group nodded their heads. It was an eclectic group. Some were bipolar, but some were recovering addicts and some had other diseases - mostly depression. All of them had spent time in an institution of some sort.

"The key here," Jen, the facilitator, said, "is that you don't let your desire to hide rule your life. It's fine to make a life change - great even. And moving to a new place is certainly a way to do that, but you have to be sure you're doing it for the right reasons - not just because you don't want to see people you've hurt."

That made sense, but it didn't stop my daydreaming.

Another part of my therapy, and sentence, was to write letters to all the people I injured. I couldn't bring myself to do this while in the institution. It was just too hard, but now my new probation officer was bearing down on me to get it done. He had a little checklist for me. When I went to a group session, he checked it off. When I went to see my psychiatrist, he checked it off. The same was true for parenting classes, meeting with my mentor, preparing a budget, and then, the letters.

I sat down one afternoon while Jack was in school and Maddie was napping. With a thick pad of paper on my lap and my favorite pen, I began to write. It started out very methodical at first, nice greetings, apologies, but soon the letters became sweeping of epics of what I had experienced, what led me to do such a horrible thing and what my life was like in the institution. I wrote seven letters, each one longer than the last and then, before I could change my mind, I sealed them and mailed them away. I couldn't imagine what kind of reaction they would get - or if they would get any reaction at all.

For days after I mailed the letters out, I waited. I waited for a phone call or a letter. I waited for someone to show up at my door and bawl me out. But nothing happened. Maybe no one cared. Maybe they made no difference to anyone at all. But they made a difference to me. As I wrote the story out on paper, I felt less ashamed - not for my crime, of course, I would always fee shame for that - but of myself. In the silent weeks that followed, I started to shop in my own town again. I took the children to events at the library and to swimming lessons at the YMCA. I felt like everyone around me was talking about me, and I looked around constantly - paranoid of who was there, but I didn't let it stop me.

I sat down at swimming lessons one day and was startled to hear my name being called. I didn't have many friends anymore, Emily being the only one who still came around and we rarely saw each other while we were out. I whipped around to see a woman named Shelby waving to me. She picked up her little one and walked over to my spot on the bleachers. I didn't know her well, but I knew she was one of the daycare center clients that I screwed. My heart pounded as she came closer.

"Hey!" she said. "How are you?"

"Um, fine," I said, very confused. "How are you?"

"Oh good. Busy and super tired," she said. "Hey, I just wanted you to know that I read your letter."

"Oh?" I said, I hadn't known it was going around.

"Yes, some of the mothers have been passing around copies. We all know it's been hard for you. I mean, what did I lose, $20? You lost a lot more and most of us know that." She talked so fast. It was all so nonchalant.

"Thanks, I guess," I said.

"Look, I just wanted you to know that. And hey, I'm having a party soon - maybe you could come?"

"Sure, maybe," I said. "That would be nice." I was hopeful, maybe this wouldn't be so bad. Maybe I could get back into my old life, but of course the invitation never came and even if it had, I wouldn't have gone.

"It's so weird," I told Emily one day over coffee. "It's like, I really wanted them to just accept me back and then I realized, I didn't."

"You shouldn't worry about it so much," she said. "You need to find your own path and new friends who accept you as you are. The PTA moms are like high school - we hated them, remember? Even if they're nice to you, they'll never see you the same. But then again, they never saw us as the same, even when you weren't a criminal." This made me smile. Emily was the only one who could call me that without me getting hurt. Michael tried to joke around like that with me sometimes and all I felt was resentment because I would always be the criminal and he would always be just the guy who got sick. He would always be the guy who was heroic for staying with me. Who took care of his family even when his wife was in the mental institution.

Shelby wasn't the only one who made a point of talking to me in those first months after I got out. Others came up to me during library storytimes and asked me what I was doing now or how I was coping. I always gave cheerful answers, determined to let them know that I would survive their anger. When they walked away from our little chats, I always got the feeling they felt they had done their good deed for the day, expressing forgiveness to the girl who had wronged them. Was it wrong of me to resent them? Maybe. But they looked so superior when they came up to me. They still had their lives intact - the same lives they had when I left. And I never belonged with them, I was fool to even try and now I was worse because I was chain-smoking mother with a record. If it hadn't been for the Lithium, I would have been really depressed about it.

About three months after I returned home, and well into my plans for escape once my probation was over, I received a visitor. Bill Thomas, my editor from the St. Elizabeth paper, appeared at my door one afternoon. Stunned, I let him in and brewed some coffee.

"Sorry for the mess," I said, cleaning up the counter. "I didn't get to the dishes yet."

"No problem," he said. "I'm still a bachelor, you know, my place is a wreck."

I sat down at the kitchen table opposite him.

"So," he said. "I'll get right to it. I read about your troubles on the wire."

"I made the wire?" I asked. Oh God, I thought, I was statewide news? This is too much.

"Well, I'm afraid that Wisconsin isn't always the most exciting state for news," he said. "Anyway, I wanted to see you sooner, but a doctor, I forget her name, at the county hospital said to wait until you got home."

"Dr. Leslie?"

"Yeah, something like that," he said. "She did mention that you were taking pictures in the hospital - do you have any of them?"

"A few," I went to the office to retrieve the small portfolio I started there. He flipped through them.

"These are good," he said. "You should publish these."

"Nah," I said. "Who would want pictures of a bunch mental patients - it was just something to do."

"No, seriously," he said. "You could do some more - at other mental hospitals or group homes and publish a series in a magazine or even a book."

"Now you sound crazier than me," I said. He laughed.

"I'll look into it for you," he said. "Anyway, back to why I'm here. I talked with the photo editor, Tim Murphy, at the Onion Bay Times, I noticed a while ago that they were looking for new photographer. I told them about you - well, what they didn't already know - and, to make a long story short, they said they'd give you a shot at a part time job if you wanted it."

"What?"

"A part time job, as a photographer," he repeated.

"No," I said. "I couldn't do that, besides, I was in their paper for weeks from what I've heard. They must think I'm nuts."

"Well, yeah," he said. "But I also showed him some of your old stuff - news photos, calendars, portraits - and he could see how talented you are."

"I'm not talented," I said.

"You are, Carrie," he said, "you just have to stop letting the other crap get in the way. Now, it doesn't pay much - like $8 an hour and it's only 20 hours or less a week, but it's something."

"But if the job was open back when I was in the institution, isn't it likely they've filled it by now?"

"Well, believe it or not, I go back a long way with Tim - we went to high school together and I convinced him to fill the job with interns until you made a decision."

"You didn't," I said.

"Yup," he said.

"God, Bill, why are you doing all of this? After everything I've done, I don't deserve…"

"Yes, you do. Everyone deserves a break Carrie and you are one of the nicest people I have ever known. What's past is past. You have to move on with your life - and you should use your talent to do it. Besides, at a newspaper, you don't have to handle any cash." He smiled and held out Tim's card.

"Ha, ha," I said, taking the card and thumbing it over. "Yeah, OK. Maybe."

"You should do it Carrie," he said. "And when you're up for it - I'll throw some freelance stuff your way - calendar pictures and that kind of stuff." He finished his coffee and got up to leave.

"Bill, I don't know how to…"

"Don't worry about it," he said. "It was a small thing for me. No big deal. I've always liked you and, well, if I was about 20 years younger…"

I gave him a hug and saw him out the door.

"I'll e-mail you about the other stuff," he said. "And we'll get those black and whites published somewhere."

"OK," I said, waving. Wow, I thought. I did still have a few friends.

Gandhi was a Libra

I spent days agonizing over whether or not to call this guy. I talked about it so much Michael finally told me to just shut up and call him. I tossed and turned every night with the prospect. On the one hand, it was very exciting. I would be a regular staff photographer again. Maddie and Jack were old enough to do without me for a while each day - heck, they'd done without me for a year and I was eager to dedicate myself to something again, not to mention contribute positively to the family income. On the other hand, my name would be in the paper every single day, under each photo I took. What if they complained? What if Phyllis, who had led the charge so voraciously against me wrote letters to the editor complaining about my presence? Besides, was it too egocentric of me to take such a public job so soon after being released? Particularly in photography? Was I throwing it in the faces of everyone I had screwed?

The guilt ate away at me. What about all of my instincts to do something for people, like being a nurse? How could taking pictures ever make up for my sins?

Dr. Oliver Maier, my new psychiatrist, told me to calm down. His office was much cleaner - much richer - than Dr. Leslie's and the smell of cat piss was noticeably absent. I had come to associate spilling my guts with that smell.

"But aren't I just going back to being the same selfish person I was if I take this job?" I asked again.

"No," he said. "You have to remember, it was not the photography that caused you to commit your crime. It was first, your illness and second, your proximity to so much cash."

"I know, but..."

"No, I don't think you do. What if you had been a cashier or a bartender or in some other position where a lot of cash was floating around?"

"I probably would have taken that."

"Yes, you see? It is your illness, not your camera, that made you commit the crime."

"You know what's weird though?"

"What's that?"

"I don't know that, even now, given the same circumstances I wouldn't do it again."

"Even with all you've been through?"

"Yeah, I mean, I knew it was wrong and I know it's wrong now and even through my diagnosis and everything else, I still think that if put in the same position, I might still do what I did."

"Really..."

"I mean, I wouldn't do it again now. But I mean, if I lived my life over and the same thing happened..."

"I see..."

"What does that mean?"

"I believe you are still, somewhere, trying to justify the action. Trying to make up for it by not being really to blame."

"That's not good," I said.

"No, it's not," he said. "But it's not unusual. You still need to come to terms - not just with your illness, but with you actions. Feeling bad and writing letters won't mean anything until you acknowledge that what you did was wrong morally and ethically."

"Maybe I have no morals."

"You do. We all do. But you have to apply them not just to everyone else, but yourself as well. This is a good topic for you to talk with your group about. Next time, let's talk about what they said."

"OK," I said, instantly regretting that I had said anything at all about it. As I got up, I also noticed I didn't feel like coughing up a furball.

It had been a long time since I applied for a job. I was nervous making the phone call to Tim and even more nervous when he actually invited me to come in. I spent the weekend before the interview going over and over my photos, trying desperately to decide which ones to include in my portfolio. I chose mainly news photos from years before, but I threw in some recent ones from the institution - no use denying where I'd been.

The office wasn't that far from my house, but I drove anyway, convinced I would fall on the sidewalk, or worse, be seen by people in the neighborhood. I was still scared to death to be seen doing anything. I pulled up in front of the newspaper office, an old Onion manse with a wooden sign in front. Walking up the front porch stairs lined with geraniums I quelled the urge to turn and run back to the car, but kept going forward somehow. Pushing open the heavy oak door, I entered the foyer and immediately smelled the familiar scent of newsprint. A girl in jeans and a sweatshirt welcomed me to the office and asked me to have a seat on the one rickety wooden chair in her reception room. She paged Tim and then was called from at least three different offices. She smiled, rolled her eyes at me and ran down the hall.

I didn't wait long. Tim Murphy appeared at the door to the office, out of breath and with a mop of gray and silver hair covering his eyes. He pushed the hair back and reached for my hand as I stood up.

"Sorry," he said. "I was outside."

"No problem," I said. "Nice to meet you."

"You too," he said. "Let's go down to the conference room." We walked down a tall hallway with peeling yellow walls and a dark wood floor that echoed my heels as I clicked down it.

He opened a door and led me into a small room with a large veneer table and pointed me to a chair. He sat opposite me and motioned for me to hand him my portfolio. As he flipped through the pages, I looked around the room. Framed front pages from at least thirty Onion Bay Times covered the walls. Packers victories and newspaper anniversaries illustrated the many changes in both font and format that the paper had gone through over the years.

"These are good," he said.

"Thanks," I said.

"Do you have any problem working nights or weekends?"

"No, not really, my mother-in-law can babysit."

"Good. And do you have a reliable car?"

"Yes?" I said, knowing full well that my vehicle wasn't always reliable.

He laughed. "Don't worry, mine's not always reliable either. We have some delivery cars that circulation uses that we can use in a pinch - as long as you can get here."

"Oh, I only live a few blocks away," I said eagerly, "I can walk if I have to."

"That's good."

"OK, then. I've already talked to your references, your work looks exceptional, why don't you come in tomorrow morning and we'll look at the equipment you already have - we haven't gone entirely digital yet, we still develop our film - and we'll work out some hours for the first couple of weeks."

"Um…OK," I said.

"Great - tomorrow then, about nine?"

And that was it. I had a job. As a photographer. No questions about my past. No wondering about my meds, nothing. I was hired. I knew it was probably a pity hiring, a favor to Bill, but I didn't care.

Chapter 19:

Two years later, I walked into the sheriff's office for the last time. The smell of stale beer and what I recognized as cardboard escorted me to the heavily secured door and the mandatory buzzer. I pushed the button and looked into the camera, waiting for them to recognize me and let me in. I walked through the door, careful to close it behind me and walked up another set of steps to the elevator. The elevator opened automatically and would only open on the second floor. I got out and sat in a wooden chair outside my probation officer's office. I had my folder with me, thick with recommendations from my employer, the parenting classes, the group sessions, my psychiatrist and even one from Emily.

The big, hulking man did not smile, as he never did, when he motioned me in. I sat in the now-familiar chair and gave him my folder. He took it silently and typed my information into the computer. Every week for two very long years I had humiliated myself by buzzing myself into this place and waiting in that elevator. I never brought the kids or Michael here. I always came alone and watched in silence as he filled out my papers, asked me about my job and my sessions and then let me go. It was he, not my parents, whom I had to call when we wanted to take a camping trip through the Upper

Peninsula of Michigan. It was he I called, not my friends, to let him know I had returned from a long weekend at Great America in Illinois.

And yet, I knew nothing about him. Many times I sat in this chair, watching him type and fill out my forms wondering how he could know everything about me, and I so little about him. I knew he liked Diet Coke and the Packers, as a can was always within reach and an autographed picture of Brett Favre was on the wall. But then, in this town, who didn't like the Packers? But that's it. That's all I knew. He, on the other hand, had been to my house, met my children and husband, knew what medication I was on, knew where I worked, what I did, where I went on vacation. It was very unnerving, but that's the price you pay for being a criminal.

This day, though, was different. On this day, he would sign my papers for the last time and as he did, I saw him get one more.

"You need to sign this here," he said, pointing to a line.

"What is it?"

"It's the certification of completion for your probation. It goes to the judge, and, assuming there are no problems, you're done."

"When will I know if there are any problems?"

"Don't worry, we'll call you, but I don't foresee any."

"That's good."

"Alright," he said. "You're done."

"Thanks," I said, extending my hand, "I appreciate it."

And then he smiled.

"Good luck to you Carrie." Carrie, he called me. I was Carrie again - not Ms. O'Connor or number 28 or whatever. I was Carrie and I was free. I walked out of that building with my head held high.

Of course, I was never truly free, but I didn't let that stop me then. I was free from the state of Wisconsin, but I was still a prisoner to my disease and my medication.

Gandhi was a Libra

I would relapse more than once over the years, but never to the extent that I had during my weakest days. I would forget to take my medication and then would be frantic over something or another. Fortunately Michael was usually around to calm me down.

I spent my first two years at the paper, during my probation, counting the days until I could leave this horrendous state, so embarrassed was I by every picture I had to take of the school board, where Phyllis was in charge or events at the children's school. But even after my probation, I continued to stay. I loved my job even though I was still nervous each time I saw a Stepford wife.

We lived in separate worlds they and I. They still stayed at home, decorating their Martha Stewart worlds and drove their brand-new Suburbans. I continued to work and lost, over time, my desire to be one of them. In my job I met more people than I could ever have imagined and I heard their stories, day after day. Everyone has a story, they say, and it's so true. People live their lives, just go about them one day at a time and sometimes good stuff happens and a lot of times really crappy stuff happens.

Life is suffering, Michael always tells me. But it's also joy and fun and love and boredom. I forgot that for a while. Illness or no, I lost touch with the idea that not everything has to be perfect. Sometimes, life just sucks and it's getting through those times, hopefully with people who love you and hopefully without committing a major crime, that makes it worthwhile.

I'll never be cured. But I'm healing and in the end, I think, that's all a person can ask for.

About the Author

Michelle Kennedy is also the author of <u>Without a Net: Middle Class and Homeless (With Kids) in America</u> published by Viking in 2005, as well as <u>The Last Straw Strategies</u>, eight books on parenting issues, published by Barron's in 2003 and 2004 and <u>It Worked for Me: 1,001 Real Life Pregnancy Tips</u>, published by Barron's in 2004.

Her work has appeared in The New York Times, Salon.com, The Christian Science Monitor, Redbook, Family Circle and many other publications.

To learn more about Michelle and her work, please visit: www.mishakennedy.com.

www.ingramcontent.com/pod-product-compliance
Lightning Source LLC
Chambersburg PA
CBHW020127180626
46810CB00004B/1440